An explosi barreling straight toward them.

A knot of terror lodged in Wyatt's throat.

"Taylor, run! Get to higher ground." He grasped his son around the waist, ignoring the pain in his injured arm. While dodging boulders raining down upon them, he held his hand over top of Levi's head. Shadow barked, and Taylor yelled into her radio, requesting assistance and a chopper evacuation.

A bullet pinged off a rock in front of Wyatt, stopping him in his tracks. He examined the cliffs. Three hunters stood on the ridge, rifles pointed in their direction.

They were pinned down. Shooters above them, falling rocks below.

Panic clawed at Wyatt, paralyzing his body as everything faded into a tunnel of chaos.

"Wyatt! Concentrate and fire back!"

Taylor's forceful tone snapped Wyatt out of his frozen state. He shielded Levi and pulled out his weapon. He fired toward the hunters, but his bullets went wide...

Darlene L. Turner is an award-winning author who lives with her husband, Jeff, in Ontario, Canada. Her love of suspense began when she read her first Nancy Drew book. She's turned that passion into her writing and believes readers will be captured by her plots, inspired by her strong characters and moved by her inspirational message. Visit Darlene at www.darleneturner.com, where there's suspense beyond borders.

Books by Darlene L. Turner

Love Inspired Suspense

National Park Protectors

Danger in the Wilderness
Trail of Mountain Secrets
Scent of Peril

Crisis Rescue Team

Fatal Forensic Investigation
Explosive Christmas Showdown
Mountain Abduction Rescue
Buried Grave Secrets
Yukon Wilderness Evidence
K-9 Ranch Protection

Love Inspired Trade

Echoes of Darkness

Visit the Author Profile page at LoveInspired.com for more titles.

SCENT OF PERIL
DARLENE L. TURNER

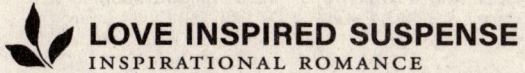

If you purchased this book without a cover you should be aware that this book is stolen property. It was reported as "unsold and destroyed" to the publisher, and neither the author nor the publisher has received any payment for this "stripped book."

ISBN-13: 978-1-335-95776-4

Scent of Peril

Copyright © 2026 by Darlene L. Turner

All rights reserved. No part of this book may be used or reproduced in any manner whatsoever without written permission.

Without limiting the exclusive rights of any author, contributor or the publisher of this publication, any unauthorized use of this publication to train generative artificial intelligence (AI) technologies is expressly prohibited. Harlequin also exercises their rights under Article 4(3) of the Digital Single Market Directive 2019/790 and expressly reserves this publication from the text and data mining exception.

This is a work of fiction. Names, characters, places and incidents are either the product of the author's imagination or are used fictitiously. Any resemblance to actual persons, living or dead, businesses, companies, events or locales is entirely coincidental.

For questions and comments about the quality of this book, please contact us at CustomerService@Harlequin.com.

® is a trademark of Harlequin Enterprises ULC.

Love Inspired
22 Adelaide St. West, 41st Floor
Toronto, Ontario M5H 4E3, Canada
www.LoveInspired.com

HarperCollins Publishers
Macken House, 39/40 Mayor Street Upper,
Dublin 1, D01 C9W8, Ireland
www.HarperCollins.com

Printed in Lithuania

He that dwelleth in the secret place of the most High
shall abide under the shadow of the Almighty.
I will say of the Lord, He is my refuge and my fortress:
my God; in him will I trust.
—*Psalm* 91:1–2

For my beautiful nieces:
Alysia, Christine, Julie, Leanne, Maddy,
Megan, Rachel and Vanessa
You bless our lives and we praise God for you!

Acknowledgments

Jesus, thank You for always being present in the storms of life. For protecting me, guiding me, and for the blessings You bestow on me every day. I love You.

Jeff, thank you for your continued support in my writing journey. I couldn't do this without you. Love you!

Tamela Hancock Murray—my agent, thank you for your unwavering support, wisdom and belief in my stories. I appreciate everything you do for me.

Tina James—my editor, thank you for your insight and encouragement. I'm so grateful for your partnership and the care you bring to every page.

A huge thank-you to Darlene's Border Patrol—your enthusiasm, early feedback and willingness to help spread the word about my books mean the world to me.

ONE

Silence blanketed the normally bustling wilderness of Teragoose National Park, Newfoundland. Odd. Conservation Officer Wyatt Hoyt adjusted his cowboy hat and steered his sorrel horse, Ember, onto the path toward Kesbush River. Multiple accounts of illegal hunting had been reported to their Labrador resource detachment near Happy Valley-Goose Bay, and Wyatt's boss had dispatched him to patrol the northern region of the park. So far, the wilderness and mountainous area had remained eerily tranquil.

Keep your eyes to the skies and ears in nature.

His father Frank Hoyt's mantra tumbled through Wyatt's head. Right now, nature's silence was telling Wyatt something was wrong in the park.

Terribly wrong.

Normally, the birds chirped, squirrels squawked and the occasional rabbit scurried across his path. However, on this midmorning June day, it seemed nature hid in the shadows. Even the normal hikers were nowhere to be seen.

Ember snorted and threw her snout in the air, halting on the narrow path.

Wyatt tensed and leaned forward to rub his horse's neck. "What is it, girl?"

She stomped her right hoof, as if in response to his question.

And Wyatt trusted Ember's animal instinct. He rested his hand on his sidearm and scanned the area, listening closely to nature for some clue why the forest had hushed.

But no answers came.

His radio crackled, disrupting the park's stillness.

"Hoyt, any sign of the hunters in your area?" fellow Conservation Officer Cam Field asked.

Wyatt unclipped his radio. "Nothing. You?"

"Nope. Only activity I've seen here in the south end is the occasional hiker and rabbit."

"I haven't seen or heard anything. It's like the park is refusing to talk today." Wyatt loved the quietness of the wilderness and being by himself, but not when all God's creations remained in the shadows. "I don't like it. Something is wrong."

"You're paranoid. I'm guessing the hunters have given up the chase and obeyed our rules."

"Doubtful. They're just getting smarter." Wyatt suspected the hunters probably only stalked their game in the dark on off-seasons.

Once again, Ember snorted and shifted positions.

"Something is spooking my horse. I don't like it."

"Cowboy, she's probably tired of you on her back." Field chuckled. "I'm doing one more pass and then I need a coffee break."

Of course you do. The man was always taking breaks. That and his flippant way of nicknaming him "cowboy" grated on Wyatt's nerves. "I'm heading to the river. Talk later."

"Copy that. Stay alert. I know how you get distracted in the forest."

Wyatt bit his tongue as his frustration toward his fellow officer emerged. Cam Field liked to ridicule everyone in his path to make himself look good, and Wyatt was tired of his disrespectful ways. Unfortunately, Field was their supervisor's favorite, and in his eyes, Cam could do no wrong.

Wyatt ignored the man's comment and sat straighter in the saddle. "Okay, girl. Enough of that. Time to head to the river." Wyatt clucked his tongue and pressed his knees into her sides.

Ember obeyed and trotted forward.

The pair traveled another five minutes before rounding the

path's bend, toward the river. The area's peaceful atmosphere and popular fishing spot were well-known.

Kesbush River was also the favorite swimming hole of Wyatt's five-year-old son. Wyatt smiled as he pictured Levi wading in the shallow water, skipping rocks. When his stone sunk without skittering across the river, Levi's pout reminded Wyatt of his late wife, Lisa, whenever she didn't get her way.

Wyatt puffed out a sigh at the same moment as Ember whinnied and reared her front legs. "Whoa, girl!" He clutched his saddle's horn with a vise grip. Falling off his horse wasn't how he wanted to start his day. "You're okay."

Ember plunked her front hooves back onto the ground, but remained at the edge of the river's path. She clearly refused to go any farther.

Wyatt brought out his binoculars and searched for whatever could have alarmed his horse. He stopped when he spied an object in the water. "What is that?" He adjusted the scope, and the item came into perfect focus.

Wyatt gasped.

A woman lay face down in the river with two arrows protruding from her back.

No wonder the forest was quiet. Someone had attacked a hiker.

Wyatt tucked his binoculars away and unhooked his radio. "Officer Hoyt here. Spotted a woman floating in the Kesbush River approximately two kilometers east of the trailhead with two arrows in her back. Send police to my location."

"Sending them now, Officer Hoyt," Dispatch said.

"Did you just say arrows?" Field asked.

"Affirmative. Heading into the river to confirm her condition." Wyatt dismounted and extracted his rifle from its holder.

"Approach with caution." Field's warning boomed through the radio.

Like I don't know that. Wyatt resisted the urge to roll his eyes at his colleague's instruction. *I know how to do my job and pro-*

tect our resources. Wyatt bit the inside of his mouth. *Don't let the man get to you.* Wyatt's fear of failure, stemming from his brother Kyle's death, flashed in his mind, but he suppressed the memory and lifted his rifle, peering through the scope. *Stay in the present.* Before approaching, he quickly observed the riverbank and tree line, searching for the killer.

Nothing suspicious materialized.

He lowered his weapon and stuffed the rifle back in its saddle holder. Removing his utility belt, he bolted toward the river and dropped it on a nearby fallen log before rushing into the water to where the woman's body slapped against a protruding rock. Wyatt turned her on her side and caught a glimpse of her face. He sucked in a breath.

Long strands of matted, dark hair covered her pale left cheek. Wyatt hauled her to the river's edge and up onto the shore. He kneeled on the rocky beach and placed his fingers on her neck, then leaned close to check her breathing. No pulse or breath. Deceased.

Wyatt sat back on his heels and hung his head, sorrow crowding his emotions. He caught a glimpse of her pink jacket and plaid shirt in his peripheral vision. He stilled, a jolt of foreboding locking him in place. Wait—he remembered similar clothing on—

"Please, no." Wyatt held his breath and pushed a strand of hair away from her neck, searching for what he prayed wasn't there.

But a butterfly tattoo appeared.

The woman was who he feared. Denise Martin—his sister-in-law—and Levi's babysitter.

Wyatt shot to his feet and searched the shoreline. Denise had mentioned taking Levi for an adventurous hike, but not in this park. So, why had she come here—and more importantly, where was his son?

His pulse skyrocketed as his shaky fingers picked up his radio and hit the button. "Deceased victim's name is—" he gulped in a breath before continuing "—Denise Martin, my son's babysitter."

"What?" Field's voice reverberated over the airway. "Where's Levi?"

"No idea. Dispatch, also send the medical examiner here and ask the police to send their K-9 unit. There's no way Denise would have left his side if she were alive. Something is wrong." He gave them a description of Levi and what his son was wearing.

"On it," Dispatch said. "I'll update you on their ETA."

"Thank you. I'm going to search for Levi." Wyatt hated to leave the body unattended, but had no choice. His son's life was at risk. He eyed Denise. "Why did you bring him here? I told you not to come to this park." His sudden spark of anger toward the woman faded as quickly as it developed. "Lisa, I'm so sorry. I failed your sister." *Lord, please help me not to fail my son, too.*

Tears prickled the back of his eyes, but he willed them to stay at bay. Tears wouldn't help his son. Wyatt hurried back to Ember. "Time to go, girl." He mounted her and squeezed his legs into her flank. Moving the reins to the left, he led Ember back into the forest as a question rose.

Should he yell Levi's name with a deadly archer in the woods? No. Even at the young age of five, Wyatt had taught his son to hide when in danger.

Wyatt couldn't risk exposing Levi. He'd have to search in silence.

"Hoyt, emergency services ETA is approximately twenty minutes out," Dispatch said. "K-9 unit is closer and on their way."

Wyatt hit his radio button. "Copy."

Ten minutes after a futile search, Wyatt pulled on Ember's reins at the Kesbush and Goosebirch Trail intersection. An item hanging on a branch caught his eye.

His son's ball cap.

A bark sounded behind him, and Wyatt pivoted.

A German shepherd emerged between the trees with its handler.

Wyatt froze, his breath catching like he'd been punched. Was he seeing correctly? He blinked rapidly to clear his vision, confirming her presence.

But there she was—Constable Taylor Grant. His ex-girlfriend. The woman who had shattered his heart and disappeared out of his life two years ago.

"What are you doing here?" Oops. The words came out harsher than Wyatt had intended. "I mean, I thought you were living in Nova Scotia."

"I moved back two weeks ago. I heard the call over the radio and your son's description. When they said 'conservation officer,' I guessed it was Levi. I raced to get here as quick as I could." Taylor tucked a stray dirty-blond curl behind her ear.

Wyatt squashed the emotions resurfacing at her reappearance. His son's life depended on him setting his feelings aside. "Thank you for coming." He pointed to the hat. "That's Levi's and my sister-in-law is lying dead on the beach with two arrows in her back. I need to find my son."

"I'm so sorry about Denise. I know you were close." She tugged on the dog's leash. "We'll use the hat to get Shadow searching."

"Okay, let's—"

Shadow barked, yanking Taylor forward.

Ember whinnied.

Green camouflage flashed in between the trees seconds before an arrow lodged into the tree above Wyatt's head.

"Take cover!" Wyatt dropped to the ground.

He was right. The forest was silent for a reason.

Hunters had invaded and demanded the territory for their own.

Bile rose at the back of Constable Taylor Grant's throat, her heartbeat thundering. She sank to one knee and brought out her Glock. Shadow continued to bark. Taylor had to not only protect Wyatt but her K-9. She wouldn't let anything happen to this dog.

Images of a similar situation from years ago rose, but she shoved them away. *Don't go there. Not here, not now.*

"Do you see the hunter?" Wyatt's elevated tone revealed his frantic emotional state.

Taylor aimed her weapon in different directions as she studied the trees. But the forest had silenced. "No, I think the archer is gone. Shadow must have scared him away."

Wyatt's gaze shifted to the arrow lodged in the tree. "Good thing because I would have been a goner." He rubbed the dog's back. "Thank you, Shadow."

The dog leaned into Wyatt's touch.

Taylor flinched at the all-too-familiar gesture. Wyatt and Shadow had been best friends before—

Don't go there either, Taylor. Her heart couldn't take it and seeing Wyatt only brought back the hurt—tenfold. *Focus.* "Tell me what happened." Taylor straightened from her crouched position, readjusted her backpack and checked the path to ensure their safety.

Wyatt explained how he'd been patrolling the area because of reports of illegal hunters when he found his sister-in-law's body floating in the river.

"Why would Denise come here? Did you suggest she go to a different park?"

His eyes clouded. "Of course I did. But if I know my son, he probably had a tantrum and convinced her to come here. He loves this park. It's his favorite place to explore. You know how he loves nature…just like his grandfather." Wyatt's voice quivered.

Taylor placed her hand on his arm. "We'll find him. Shadow is the best at what he does."

"I'm counting on that. I can't lose Levi, too."

Taylor knew exactly what Wyatt was referring to. His wife, Lisa, had died in a car accident when Levi was only one. Wyatt took her death hard and confessed he struggled to date even after two years had passed. But he took a risk with Taylor, and she ended up breaking his heart all over again.

But it couldn't be helped. He deserved someone better than her. Someone who could give him what he wanted.

Lots of children.

But she couldn't, thanks to her cancer. The chemo and hysterectomy had taken everything from her, including her dream of becoming a mother.

Get your head in the game. She stood quickly and brushed the dirt from her uniform with her right hand, keeping the weapon in her left raised in case of any danger.

Shouts along the path drew her attention. "That's probably the medical examiner. I have to give a situation report to the others."

After being assured the threat had passed, Taylor holstered her weapon and gestured toward the branch. "Then we'll use Levi's hat and Shadow will find him." At least, she prayed that would happen.

Wyatt's contorted expression told her he may crumble at any moment and she would do anything to prevent him from being separated from his son.

"Thank you." He smiled. "It's truly good to see you again."

"You, too." Taylor pressed her radio button and gave an update to her team, describing the attack. "Going to get Shadow searching."

"Keep us updated, Constable Grant," Sergeant Mitchell said. "Be safe. We're hearing rumblings of a weapon smuggling ring across the province."

Wyatt drew in a sharp breath. "Could that be why someone killed Denise? She came across them?"

"Possibly, but let's not go there." She pressed her radio button again. "Sergeant, any details on that ring?"

"Nothing. New information as of thirty minutes ago. Take all precautions."

"Copy."

A lanky man bounded around the corner. "Hoyt, you catch the hunter? Why aren't you searching, Cowboy?" The man's tone conveyed sarcasm, as if implying incompetence.

Taylor didn't miss Wyatt's scowl. Heat flushed her cheeks as anger bubbled to the surface. One thing Taylor hated was a bully.

And this man appeared to fit that description.

Beside her, Shadow growled.

Seemed her dog agreed with Taylor's assessment.

"Who are you?" she asked.

The man's eyes traveled across her uniform, settling on the police patch on her coat. "Conservation Officer Cam Field. You are?"

"Constable Taylor Grant from the West Newfoundland Constabulary." She gathered her dog's leash. "And this is Shadow. We're here to assist Officer Hoyt in finding his son."

Wyatt cleared his throat and pointed to the arrow. "We were about to get started when we were attacked, so I'd appreciate it if you give us a break."

Shadow barked.

Taylor's hand flew to her mouth, attempting to hide the emerging grin. Her dog agreed with Wyatt's statement.

The conservation officer crossed his arms, but remained silent.

Good idea, you don't want to see the wrath of Shadow.

Dr. Julia Oke and her assistant approached the group. "Can one of you direct me to the female's body?"

Officer Field uncrossed his arms and leaned close. "Cowboy, you don't have to be so touchy," he whispered before addressing the medical examiner. "Dr. Oke, I'll take you to the shoreline." He waved to the right. "This way."

Dr. Oke and her employee proceeded down the path.

Field glanced over his shoulder. "I'll take over from here, Cowboy. You continue with your search. The park warden and constables have others coming to help." He sauntered toward the river.

"He's interesting." Taylor lifted the ball cap from the branch with her gloved hand.

"You don't know the half of it. He's a brownnoser and likes to make me look bad." Wyatt dug his boot into the dirt. "I'm surprised he got here so fast. He was searching for the hunters farther south."

"I'm sorry you have to work with someone like that. I have a few of those in our station, too." She squatted in front of Shadow, holding out the hat. "Let's forget about him and get my dog searching."

The K-9 sniffed.

"Shadow, seek!" She unclipped his leash and tucked it into her pocket.

The German shepherd raised his head, nostrils flaring in the breeze as he locked onto a scent, and sniffed methodically along the tree line's edge, paws silent on the damp earth. With a sudden surge of purpose, he veered onto the path, barreling in a northerly direction, his tail high and ears alert, tracking with needlelike focus.

"He's caught a whiff of something. Follow him." Taylor dashed after her dog while keeping her senses on alert for the archer and any other intruders.

Behind her, galloping hooves echoed along the forest's trail. She turned at Wyatt's approach.

He slowed his horse and reached his hand down. "Get on. We'll be faster keeping up with Shadow on Ember."

She grabbed his hand, and he hoisted her upward onto his horse. Taylor wrapped her arms around his back. She'd forgotten the strength of this cowboy turned conservation officer.

Seconds later, they came to a fork in the path.

Wyatt tugged on the reins. "Which way did he go? Shadow is fast."

Taylor looked left, then right. A flash of russet combined with black and tan leaped into the woods some distance down the trail. She pointed right. "There he is. Go!"

Wyatt clucked and Ember lurched forward, following the dog.

Seconds later, the horse halted, rearing backward.

Taylor lost her hold and slipped, her breath catching in her throat.

Wyatt seized her hand as she teetered on the edge, steadying her back onto the saddle with a firm grip.

Ember dropped her front hooves and settled.

Wyatt turned to Taylor. "You okay?"

"Yes, that was close. What spooked your horse?" Taylor wiggled out of his hold and swung her leg over the horse's rump, dismounting.

"No idea. She's been skittish today." Wyatt rubbed Ember's back. "What's gotten into you, girl?"

A bark sounded to their right.

"Shadow's found something." Taylor scanned the trees, searching for her dog. "There!" She pointed. "Let's go."

She didn't wait for Wyatt, but ducked under a cluster of low-lying branches and stepped into the woods.

Movement behind her revealed Wyatt had followed.

Taylor had lost sight of her dog. *Where are you, boy?* "Shadow, speak," Taylor yelled.

The shepherd's bark was deeper into the forest than Taylor first thought.

"Where did he go?" Wyatt asked.

Another bark answered his question, followed by a series of intense, high-pitched barks.

Something was wrong.

Again, a flash of fur caught Taylor's attention. "There." She pointed and headed left.

The duo caught up to Shadow, and the cause of his distressed barking.

Taylor's jaw dropped, her heart racing.

A man lay on the ground beside a fallen tree with a gunshot wound to his chest, a knife still clutched in his hand—and a message carved into the log.

Run!

Taylor's heart thundered, shoving her panic levels into overdrive.

Shadow growled.

Flashes of camouflage skulked in the trees seconds before a gunshot echoed throughout the woods.

The archer had brought reinforcements into their forest, elevating the danger.

TWO

Wyatt unleashed his sidearm and sunk to the ground at the base of an aspen tree with his gun raised. Tension corded his neck muscles, his entire body seizing at the thought of another attack in his park.

Taylor and Shadow sought refuge at Wyatt's right. "I'm guessing those are hunters. Did you see how many are out there?" She clutched her dog's collar.

He peered around the trunk, searching for movement in the forest. Branches rustled to his left, center and right. "I count three. Not good. We're outnumbered."

"No, we're not. We have Shadow. He's more than a search and rescue dog. That makes us a team of three." She pressed her radio button. "Taking gunfire here with Conservation Officer Hoyt and Shadow. Deceased male at the scene. Send backup to our location. Approximately three klicks from the river."

"Deploying now," a voice announced over the airwaves. "Stay put, Constable Grant. Help is coming."

"Hoyt, on my way." Field's breathy voice revealed he was running.

Great. A trigger-happy Cam Field was all they needed.

Wyatt pushed his talk button. "Approach carefully. Three armed hunters in the trees."

"Who's the deceased male?" Field asked.

Wyatt averted his gaze toward the victim, noting the unevenness of his legs. One appeared longer than the other. "No idea. Never seen him before." An item a few yards away from the body caught Wyatt's attention. Something he missed when they first approached the area.

And the reason Shadow had alerted to the crime scene.

A tiny firetruck—Levi's favorite toy.

Wyatt was trapped behind a tree, surrounded by three angry hunters, with his son somewhere hidden in the forest. He had to save Levi before the unthinkable happened. Wyatt eased himself into a standing position.

"What are you doing?" Taylor's hushed question boomed in the silent forest.

"I can't just sit and do nothing." He gestured toward the truck. "That's Levi's. He was here and I have to find him."

She nodded and pushed herself up. "Shadow, protect!"

The dog darted from his hiding position and zigzagged to the left.

A gunshot rang out, echoing in the forest. The bullet slammed into the tree where Wyatt took refuge mere inches from his head. He dropped to one knee, firing a shot toward the hunter to the right.

The man ducked behind a cluster of bushes.

Shadow barked as a flash of fur hurtled into the air. The dog had reached one hunter, protecting Wyatt and Taylor by bringing the suspect to the ground.

The male cursed. "Get him off me!"

"Shadow, hold," Taylor yelled from her position. "Wyatt, do you see the others?"

He pointed to the bushes. "One is hiding there. Lost sight of the other."

"Ridge, where are you?" The other hunter yelled into a radio. "Darn dog got Mort, and I'm pinned down. Send help."

Ridge? Was that a last name?

Shouts resonated throughout the park. Help was arriving.

Just in time.

"Ridge, did you hear me?"

Seemed this Ridge had abandoned the others.

Wyatt rose and pointed his gun toward the bushes. "Your

buddy is gone. Shadow has your friend, and now you're surrounded. Give it up."

"Never!" The man emerged from the bushes, shooting at them.

Taylor returned fire, hitting him square in the chest.

The hunter dropped, his lifeless eyes staring at the sky.

One down. One gone. The other detained by Shadow. How many more hunters lurked in Teragoose National Park?

"Wyatt, you okay?" Taylor's elevated voice revealed her heightened emotions.

"Yep. You?"

"Good. Cover me. Heading toward Shadow."

Wyatt eased out from behind the tree, tightening his grip on his 9mm. "Stand down! It's over." He laced his command with force—demanding surrender.

The only response from the captured hunter was a series of strained grunts as he struggled beneath Shadow's unrelenting grip.

Taylor charged forward, her Glock lifted and ready, her focus locked on the prisoner.

Wyatt flanked her, his senses alert and scanning the shadows for any concealed threats.

They reached Shadow, who had perched himself on top of the hunter, his jaws clenched around the man's arm, securing him in place with painstaking precision.

"Get him off," the man hissed.

"Don't be a baby. Shadow is trained to restrain but not to bite hard unless I order him to." Taylor moved in front of the hunter. "Wyatt, keep your gun raised while I cuff him."

Wyatt leveled his gun at the assailant, cementing his stance. "Got you. Go ahead."

She secured her weapon and removed cuffs from her duty belt. "Shadow, out."

The dog obeyed.

"On your back, hands behind your head."

The man sneered.

Wyatt waved his gun. "Do it. Now. Trust me, you don't want the lady to tell you twice."

This time, he complied.

Taylor cuffed him and hauled him to his feet. "Thanks for the assist, Wyatt." She turned to her dog, snapped her fingers, waving toward the man. "Shadow, hold."

The dog growled, baring his teeth, and skulked closer.

The man's eyes widened. "Keep that dog away from me." He addressed Wyatt. "Your last name Hoyt?"

Wyatt flinched, but kept his weapon aimed at the hunter. "Who's asking?"

He sneered. "You must be that kid's father."

Wyatt marched into the man's personal space. "Where is my son?"

"No idea."

Wyatt thrust his gun's barrel into the man's temple. "Tell me."

"Wyatt. Calm down." Taylor's soft voice commanded attention. "I know you want to find Levi, but that's not the way to do it and you know it."

The vein in Wyatt's neck throbbed, elevating his blood pressure, but he kept a tight hold on his gun.

"Wyatt." Taylor's single forced word brought Wyatt out of his enraged stupor.

He lowered his weapon. "You're right, but if he moves, I'll shoot."

"Cowboy, put your gun away." Field's sarcastic command bellowed behind them.

Wyatt turned.

Cam Field had his weapon aimed at the hunter. "We've got this."

Two constables approached.

Taylor withdrew Shadow's leash and hooked it to his collar,

speaking to the suspect. "Mort, who's the leader of your band of hunters?"

Wyatt returned his focus back on to the hunter. "Is it Ridge?"

The man's face darkened. "How do you know that name?"

"Your buddy hunter…who's dead by the way…called it out earlier. Who's Ridge?" Wyatt stowed his gun.

"Someone you should fear, especially if Ridge has your son."

Wyatt's mouth went dry at the thought of Levi in the hands of a madman. "Tell us more."

"Did you kill the woman we found floating in the river?" Field asked.

"Her name was Denise, Field. Denise Martin."

Field's eyes narrowed. "Simmer down, Cowboy." He returned his attention to the hunter. "Answer the question or we'll let this dog loose again."

The man's expression morphed into one of terror. "Ridge did. He's the archer and rarely misses his target."

"Why kill her?" Wyatt asked.

"Because she took something Ridge wants back. That's all I'm telling you. I value my life, and trust me, no one betrays Ridge and lives to tell about it." His lips clamped into an impregnable line.

Clearly, they would get nothing else out of the hunter.

Wyatt dug his nails into his palms, attempting to curb the alarm overtaking every region of his body.

Levi's life was in jeopardy.

And they were running out of time.

Taylor didn't miss the alarm on Wyatt's tortured face. They had to find Levi before he unraveled and did something he'd regret. Not that she'd ever seen him lose his temper, but his boy's life was at stake. Any parent in his predicament would have rage flowing through their body.

Even so, she must keep him calm in order to find Levi. But

first, she had to update her fellow constables and hand the scene over to them.

Seventy-five minutes after her colleagues escorted the prisoner to the police station, the medical examiner had transported the bodies of Denise Martin and the other victim out of the park. Forensics had also secured the scene, and Wyatt entrusted Ember into Field's care. With everything in place, the trio was ready to search for Levi Hoyt. So far, none of the other searchers had spotted any signs of the boy.

Wyatt shared how he hated to leave his horse and truck with Cam Field, but they didn't have a choice. Shadow was leading them deeper into the brush and rocky steep trails, where it would be too hard for a horse to follow. Field promised to return Ember to Wyatt's trailer and then to Wyatt's small ranch twenty minutes outside of the park. Taylor offered to drive Wyatt—and Levi—home.

She only hoped she could fulfill that promise by finding his son.

Right now, Wyatt stood behind the police caution tape, staring at the spot where the deceased male's body had been. He dropped to his hands and knees, sticking his face close to the ground.

"What are you doing?" Taylor asked.

He stared at her from his position. "I'm studying the scene from a different angle. Closer to Levi's point of view."

"Are you a tracker now?"

"Not exactly, but just doing what my father taught me. Keeping my eyes and ears in nature. He says it helps."

She squatted. "What do you see?"

He pointed to the firetruck. "Tiny footprints where he dropped his toy." He waggled his finger toward a cluster of firs. "They lead into the bush instead of toward the main path."

"Good eye." Taylor examined the indentations from Levi's feet. "Looks like he's wearing hiking boots. What else would he have with him?"

Wyatt pushed himself up, brushing dirt and leaves from his pants. "His superhero backpack with granola bars, water, flashlight, a few toys, and probably some paper and crayons."

Taylor stood, tilting her head in confusion. "Does he always hike with all that gear?"

Wyatt shrugged. "What can I say? I like to be prepared for anything just in case he gets bored. I hope he still has his bag."

"We haven't seen it anywhere, so that's a positive." She brought out Levi's hat from her backpack. "Let's get Shadow searching again."

He latched on to her hand. "Thank you for helping me. I know we didn't end things on the best of terms, but I'm grateful you're here. Please find my son."

She examined his expression and noted his sincerity. Had he forgiven her for breaking his heart? When she first met the conservation officer at a law enforcement training seminar two and a half years ago, she promised herself not to fall for Wyatt. But she failed. He was everything she'd ever wanted in a man. Kind. Trustworthy. Loyal. And…handsome in a cowboy hat. But he was also a widower with a son. She told herself it would only be a few dates. She couldn't get involved with any man. But she fell hard—and fast. They dated for two months and when he shared his desire for more children, she knew it was time. Time to do the unthinkable—break his already-fragile heart. Thankfully, a job opened up in Nova Scotia and she used that as her excuse to end whatever relationship they had. She hated herself—and still did—for what she'd done.

Taylor swallowed the thickening in her throat to both compose herself and suppress the memory of what they once had. "I will do everything I can to find Levi." She squeezed his hand. "We're in this together."

She locked gazes with Wyatt for a New York minute. *Do. Not. Go. There.* His green eyes were her kryptonite—her undoing. *Walk away.*

Taylor dropped his hand and turned to Shadow, holding the hat under his nose. "Shadow, seek!"

The K-9 sniffed the ball cap and then trotted to the trees on their right, smelling the ground in all directions. He barked and hurtled between the bushes, following Levi's tiny boot prints.

"Levi's scent is still fresh. That's a good sign. Come on!" Taylor didn't wait for a response, but parted the bushes and trailed after her dog.

Five minutes later, Shadow barked and sat beside a cluster of rocks.

"Why's he stopping?" Wyatt asked.

"He's alerted to something, but I don't see any signs of Levi. Search the area." Taylor squatted to Shadow's level to look from a dog's angle. She did a one-eighty scan, but nothing materialized.

She stood. "What is it, Shadow?"

The dog barked and shifted to the right.

"Wait, what's that?" Wyatt pointed to a depression in the grass where Shadow's paw had left a mark.

Taylor picked it up. "It's a granola bar wrapper." She handed it to him.

Wyatt's mouth hung open. "And that's the brand I buy." He circled, gazing in all directions. "Levi must be here somewhere."

"Or was earlier, but if he's lost, wouldn't he stay in one spot?"

Wyatt shook his head. "Not if he was running away from someone. If that's the case, he's leaving us clues." He held up the wrapper. "And this is the third. The ball cap was the first one, then the firetruck."

"Smart boy. And he's only five?"

"Yep, but he's a mature five-year-old. His grandfather made sure of that after Lisa passed." Wyatt puffed out a breath. "Dad spent time with us after her funeral. Then came every summer for weeks at a time to help *climatize* his Hoyt grandson." He emphasized *climatize*.

"Your father taught all your siblings about nature, didn't he?"

"Yes, and we all have some type of vocation in the wilderness. Frank Hoyt was tough on us kids, but it was for a reason. In his words, 'Nature is beautiful, but can also be deadly if you don't know what you're doing.' He wanted to toughen us all up, including his grandkids." He handed her the wrapper. "Can we use this to continue searching?"

"We'll use both." She held the items under Shadow's nose. "Seek!"

The dog raced through the underbrush, with Taylor and Wyatt at his heels.

After ten minutes of trailing Shadow, Taylor stopped and raised her fisted hand, indicating for Wyatt to halt.

His jaw dropped, confusion distorting his face, but he still complied.

"Do you hear that?" she whispered.

Mumbled voices sounded to their left.

"More hunters?" Taylor placed her hand on her weapon.

"Doubtful." Wyatt parted some branches and peered through the window he'd created. "Hunters don't talk that loud. Probably hikers or searchers."

"Where did the little guy go?" a female voice asked. "We have to find him in order to collect."

Taylor bristled. What did she mean by "collect"?

Shadow barked continuously.

"Wait, is that a dog? Here all by himself? He must be lost. Let's go get him. I've always wanted one." Pounding footfalls racing through the brush and fallen leaves boomed in the forest.

"Whoever they are, they won't get my dog." Taylor ducked under the branches and sprinted toward her K-9.

Seconds later, Taylor and Wyatt reached Shadow's location ahead of the hikers. The dog was sitting beside a hollowed-out tree trunk.

"What did he find?" Wyatt hustled forward.

Taylor inched closer. "It looks like Levi took refuge here." She pointed to a freshly eaten apple core, and a crumpled up piece of paper. Before they could examine it, a sharp crack echoed to their left.

Taylor unholstered her Glock. "Police, stand down."

Wyatt drew his gun, providing a unified front.

A male and female halted, raising their hands. "Whoa now," the male said. "We were only following a kid when we heard the dog bark."

"Yeah, and you said you always wanted a dog." Taylor gestured toward Shadow's vest. "This is my partner, and he's not for the taking."

The female's eyes enlarged. "We didn't know. Sorry."

Wyatt stepped forward. "Are you hunting in the park or are you members of the search party?"

"No. Do we look like we're hunting?" The male's sarcastic question came out loud and clear.

He was annoyed.

"You can lower your guns," the female said.

"We will." Taylor spoke to Wyatt. "Check them for weapons, just in case."

He stowed his gun and searched them. "Nothing."

"Told you. Why so jumpy?"

Wyatt seized the male by the collar. "Two people died in the forest today, and a child is missing. You best watch your attitude."

Shadow growled at Wyatt's elevated voice. He sensed the officer's heightened trepidation.

The female's hand flew to her mouth, letting out a cry. "That's terrible."

"Did either of you see any hunters in the forest?" Wyatt tightened his grip.

"No!" they said simultaneously.

But a little too quick for Taylor's liking. "Easy, Wyatt. Friends, what are your names?"

"I'm Kevin. This is Paula."

Taylor tucked her Glock into its gun sheath. "I heard you say earlier that you saw a little boy. When was this and where?"

Wyatt released Kevin and retreated to Taylor's side.

"About thirty minutes ago," Paula said. "Here on the path. The boy was by himself and we wanted to help, but when he saw us, he ran back into the bushes." She averted her gaze to Kevin.

He flicked a stray leaf off his jacket, ignoring Paula. "We tried to find him, but it's like he disappeared. Why is he in the forest by himself?"

Something about their expressions niggled at Taylor.

"Long story," Wyatt replied. "He's my son and we're trying to find him."

"And Shadow alerted to something here." Taylor squatted in front of the tree and fished out her latex gloves, putting them on. She smoothed out the crumpled paper. "It's a sketch, Wyatt."

"Let me see." He leaned over her shoulder.

And drew in a ragged, audible breath.

It was a rough drawing of a red bridge, a stick figure with an angry face holding a bow and arrow, and an unfinished airplane. A small *L* was etched in the corner.

Levi had left them a clue, but what did it mean?

Paula leaned closer. "Did Levi draw that?"

Taylor tensed, her earlier suspicion confirmed. She eyed Wyatt. He, too, caught the female's slip.

Shadow let out a low-rumbled growl.

How did she know the boy's name?

Something was definitely off about this couple.

And Taylor would get to the bottom of whatever that was.

Levi's life depended on it.

THREE

Taylor sprang to her feet and rested her left hand on her weapon. With her right, she flicked her fingers at Shadow. A command she taught him when she required him to protect and—intimidate.

The K-9 growled louder this time, baring his teeth as he moved in front of Taylor and Wyatt.

The couple shuffled backward. "Hey man, what gives?" Kevin asked.

"If you're not part of the search party, how did you know my son's name?" Wyatt stomped into Paula's personal space, the outrage in his question betraying his emotional state.

Wyatt's earlier expression had morphed into a mix of contempt, anger, and terror. Taylor imagined the tightly coiled spring would snap at any moment.

And no one could blame him. His son's life was at stake, and this couple knew something.

"Don't lie to us or I'll unleash my dog's protective skills on you. You mentioned earlier about collecting something. What did you mean? We heard you, so don't lie." Taylor placed both hands on her hips, reinforcing her threatening stance.

Kevin scowled. "Don't tell them anything, Paula."

Her lips trembled. "The hunter told me to find Levi, or he'd kill Kevin."

Taylor faced Wyatt. "How does the hunter know your son's name?"

"No idea. Perhaps Denise let it slip." He returned his attention to Paula. "Can you describe the man?"

She shook her head. "He was dressed in camouflage, wore a bandana over his mouth, and sunglasses."

"Sunglasses in a dark forest and you didn't find that strange?" Their story didn't make sense to Taylor. "Why would he ask for you to find Levi?"

Paula hung her head. "The only thing I can think of is because I'm a woman. Maybe he thought Levi would come for me. And—"

"And he promised us two thousand dollars if we helped," Kevin added.

Wyatt took off his hat and rubbed his forehead. "So, he threatened you and offered a reward? That's highly unlikely. What aren't you telling us?"

"Good question. I agree with Officer Hoyt. Tell us what detail you're leaving out of your story or I'll arrest you for trespassing." Not that Taylor could since they were in a national park open to the public, but a little pressure might help the situation.

Kevin threw his hands in the air. "Fine. He didn't really threaten us. My girlfriend here likes to embellish."

"Kev, baby. Why take the fun out of my story?" She smirked.

"So you would blatantly lie to a police officer?" Wyatt shifted his position and clutched Paula's arm. "With my son's life at risk? Tell us the truth this time."

"Fine." She wiggled out of Wyatt's hold. "We saw your son on the path moments before this hunter approached us, offering money to get Levi to trust me. But it wasn't two thousand like Kevin said, it was five thousand. We needed the money."

"She's telling the truth." Kevin addressed Taylor. "Constable, can we go now? We did nothing wrong."

Taylor's eyes rested on Paula and she clenched her hands into fists, resisting the urge to wipe the smirk off the woman's face. "Show me your identifications in case we need to contact you further."

They complied.

Taylor jotted down their names and addresses.

"We're wasting time here, Taylor." Wyatt retreated from the

female hiker. "Let's get Shadow searching again. It's getting late and my son is probably terrified."

Taylor pointed toward the trail. "Get out of the park. Now. If I see either of you again, I *will* arrest you." She unhooked her radio. "Or do I need to call in your descriptions to my team and ask them to detain you if they catch you in the park?"

Kevin raised his hands before nudging Paula through the bush. "We're going. I truly hope you find your son. That hunter didn't sound like he was messing around." He didn't wait for a response, but traipsed after his girlfriend.

Taylor prayed she hadn't just let a suspect go, but in the end, they didn't flinch when they finally admitted everything. Her gut was telling her this time they told the truth.

But remember, your gut isn't always right.

She silenced her inner voice. Now wasn't the time to go *there*.

Taylor approached Wyatt, who was kneeling in front of his son's drawing. "Can you make any sense of what Levi drew?"

"It's pretty rough, but even though Levi is five, he's always been good at drawing." Wyatt pointed to the bridge. "There are no red bridges in the park." His finger hovered over the airplane. "But there is a remote airstrip approximately ten kilometers from here. Can you have some constables deployed there to look for Levi? Just in case…"

His voice trailed off, but Taylor guessed what he was going to say. In case Ridge had kidnapped and taken his son there. She squeezed his shoulder. "Don't even think that. I will make the call, and also check on the others searching for Levi." She spoke into her radio and got an update, but so far, Wyatt's son remained missing. She requested someone check the airstrip, then report back to her. She had to relieve Wyatt's mind in any way possible. "Okay, done. Let's keep searching."

Wyatt stood. "Can we take the picture?"

She studied the skies.

Dark clouds had ushered into the area, confirming what she'd read on their local weather network earlier. A storm was headed their way, and she had to protect the evidence. "Looks like those clouds are about to give way, so we don't want it destroyed." She put on her gloves again and picked up the drawing, gingerly folding it, before placing the sketch into her coat pocket.

"Let's keep moving. I need to find my son. He hates thunderstorms." Wyatt bit his lip, his eyebrows wrinkling into worry.

And melting Taylor's heart. She hated to see him this way.

She swallowed the lump forming in her throat and commanded Shadow to seek. *Keep focused, girl. You have a job to do. Find Levi. Nothing else.* Even if the man's angst had torn at her resolve to compartmentalize her former feelings for the conservation officer.

Shadow sniffed around the hollowed-out trunk in all directions before leaping through the trees and back onto the crushed-stone path.

Wyatt and Taylor followed the dog as he stuck his nose into different parts of the wilderness and out onto the rugged trail.

"Wait." Taylor stopped and eased out Levi's drawing, unfolding it from the edges.

Wyatt halted. "What is it?"

She pointed to the bow and arrow. "Do you think he saw the hunter's weapon?"

Wyatt leaned closer, studying the picture. "Levi is fascinated with archery right now, but that's not normally how he draws them. Look at the jagged edges. Odd."

Taylor's earlier conversation with her sergeant popped into her head. "Wyatt, remember my sergeant mentioned an illegal smuggling group earlier? The constabulary has caught wind of a growing ring operating out of this part of the province." Taylor pictured the deceased male they'd found a few hours ago. "I'm guessing, but I'm curious if maybe Denise and Levi stumbled upon a deal gone bad. Perhaps they witnessed something they shouldn't have."

"I've been wondering that, too, but I haven't heard of weapons being smuggled recently, only that hunters have been hunting out of season." Wyatt's eyes widened. "Are you thinking they saw this Ridge kill the man we found?"

"I hate to suggest it, but yes."

"If that's the case, and Levi did witness that, he's in more danger than I originally thought." Wyatt kicked at a pile of leaves, scattering rocks in all directions.

Great. She didn't mean to add to the man's stress level, but she had to ask. He knew the area better than she did. "Any ideas on where they'd conduct their business, like abandoned cabins or buildings in the forest?"

"Lots. Plus caves. What type of weapons?"

She held her hands out, palms up. "Not sure. Sergeant Mitchell didn't give me any indication. It's new information, and he's assigning constables to investigate. Let's keep—"

Shadow barked a few feet from their location.

"He's found something. Come on." Taylor jogged toward her dog, with Wyatt close behind.

They rounded a bend in the path and froze at what Shadow sat beside.

A cracked cell phone lodged between two small rocks next to the tree line.

Wyatt pointed, interrupting her silent questions. "That's Denise's phone. I recognize the pink case because I gave it to her last Christmas."

Had Levi dropped it or placed it there on purpose as his next clue?

Shadow barked and trotted into the forest's edge.

Wyatt motioned toward the low-lying branch next to Shadow. "Is that—"

Taylor shifted her gaze—and understood why Wyatt's question had silenced.

Blood splattered the leaves and the ground, trailing into the woods.

Shadow turned from his position and barked before heading into the brush.

Thunder growled in the distance, its brooding warning deepening their already dangerous predicament.

Right now, Taylor ignored the weather and concentrated on the man before her. "Wyatt, it may not be Levi's blood, but we have to follow Shadow. He's alerting to something else. We can't leave the phone behind, as the rain will tamper with the evidence." Taylor hastily put on her latex gloves and took pictures of the scene, then scooped up the phone, tucking it into her backpack. "Let's go."

Taylor entered the opposite side of the forest they'd searched earlier and trampled after her dog, unleashing her sidearm.

She wasn't about to take any risks—not with a cold-blooded killer lurking nearby, determined to hunt a child and ready to silence anyone who stood in their way.

Wyatt bit the inside of his mouth, attempting to silence the terror raging through his mind at the idea of Levi hurt and alone in a dangerous forest with a storm brewing. Not to mention a deadly archer stalking him. Had Levi indeed witnessed a murder? *Lord, if You're out there, please protect Levi.* Although Wyatt had gone through the motions of attending church throughout his younger years, he failed to surrender to his parents' God. Much to his mother's dismay. Erica Hoyt was the prayer warrior of the Hoyt family, often found on her knees beside her bed at all hours—day and night—surrendering each child to God for safekeeping. *Mom, I could use those prayers right now.*

The blood trail had tapered off, giving Wyatt hope that if it was Levi who'd been injured, perhaps he simply cut his finger on something in the forest.

Shadow's bark brought Wyatt's focus out of his thoughts and back to their search.

"I think he's alerted to something again." Taylor sidestepped a large rock and plunged ahead toward her dog.

Wyatt sprinted after her as his radio crackled.

"Cowboy, back at your ranch," Field said. "Ember is safe and sound in the barn. Found Levi yet? What's your ETA?"

Wyatt unhooked his radio and spoke as he bypassed a fallen log. "Still searching."

"It's getting dark as the storm is moving in. Gonna be a messy one. You best find your son and get out of the forest."

No pressure.

Wyatt stopped and peered ahead, but lost track of where Taylor went. "Thanks for taking Ember back. Can you get a ride home?"

"Already called my wo-man." He elongated the word *woman* in a disrespectful tone.

Wyatt stiffened at the man's blatant reference to his girlfriend.

"Wyatt, over here." Taylor's shout bellowed through the woods.

"Listen, I gotta run." Wyatt didn't wait for a reply from Field, but hooked his radio back onto his waist and continued forward. "Taylor, where are you?"

"Another few feet to your left."

Wyatt veered toward the sound of her voice, hurrying to discover what Shadow found but failed to see the protruding branch. It caught him in the face. He ignored the sting and kept pushing forward.

"Over here." Her cry came from behind a row of pines.

Wyatt dodged another branch and entered a small clearing.

Shadow sat beside a large rock surrounded by bushes. Taylor had squatted beside him, examining a pile of leaves with her gloves on.

"What is it?" Wyatt approached, holding his breath.

A wad of bloodstained tissues was nestled in the leaves beside an empty water bottle and other items.

Three of Levi's toy cars in a trail, heading north.

"He's hurt." Wyatt dropped to the ground.

Taylor placed her hand on his shoulder. "Let's not go there. He probably hurt a finger or something." She pointed to the wad of tissues. "I looked at those and it appears like the one on top has less blood, so I believe he must have stopped his bleeding. He's okay, Wyatt."

She was right. Taylor had to be right. Levi was fine.

He. Was. Fine.

He has to be.

Wyatt recited the mantra in his head, willing it to be true, and pushed himself into a standing position.

"What do you make of the trail of cars?" Taylor asked.

He observed how his son had positioned the toys. "There's no way he would have dropped or parted with these on purpose. They are his favorite cars. He's telling us something."

"But what?" Taylor walked around the trail, gesturing toward the edge of the small clearing—the same direction the cars pointed. "What's over there?"

Wyatt tapped his chin and did a one-eighty to get his bearings. Then stilled. "Kesbush Cave. He must be hiding in there. We've been to that cave plenty of times, so he would know the way."

Her jaw dropped. "Are you sure your son is only five years old?"

"Yep." Wyatt smiled, pride filling every ounce of his body. He had heard those words multiple times from different people. "He can read at a first grade level, too. The way his mind works astonishes me, but I can't take the credit. It's all Frank Hoyt."

"I don't believe that. I've seen you around Levi, remember?" She snapped her fingers and pointed north. "Shadow, seek!"

The dog hurtled over the cluster of bushes and sped across the small clearing before retreating into the forest.

Fat raindrops splatted on top of the rock.

Wyatt examined the sky. "Storm is coming. We must hurry. Can you gather the cars? He'll want them."

"Of course." She scooped them up and placed them in her backpack.

He beckoned her forward. "Come on. The cave is this way."

The rain intensified as they approached the cave's entrance five minutes later. Shadow sat beside the opening, barking.

Wyatt fished out his flashlight from his pack and turned it on. "I'll go first. I'm trained in case there are bears inside. The last thing we need is to find cubs and their mama."

She removed her Maglite. "Wyatt, I'm trained, too. We're doing this together."

He cringed at the annoyance in her tone. "Sorry, didn't mean anything by that. I'm just on edge."

Taylor turned on her light. "I understand."

Together, they entered the cave and shone their lights throughout the area.

Thankfully, no bears were in the small cave.

But neither was Levi.

Wyatt slumped against the stone wall. "I thought for sure he'd be here. I've failed my son. Failed Lisa."

Taylor wrapped her arms around Wyatt. "Don't do that to yourself. You did not fail Levi or Lisa."

He clung to her and sobbed, hating the emotions overtaking him.

She rubbed his back. "We'll find him. He led us here for a reason."

Wyatt regained his composure and retreated from her embrace. "You're right. We used to play hide-and-seek in this area. I'd always find him here, and he knew that."

"Well, then, something caused him to leave his favorite hiding spot."

Shadow sprang up on all fours, his ears flattened seconds

before he let out a low growl, his gaze focused on the cave's entrance.

"What is it, boy?" Taylor stood in the opening, shining her light. "The storm has made it darker out. We have to keep going."

"What is Shadow alerting to?"

"Maybe the storm, or someone is watching." She kneeled in front of her K-9. "Seek!"

The dog bounded out of the cave, heading back the way they'd come.

Taylor bolted to her feet. "Let's go."

They dodged through the forest despite the pounding rain, chasing after Shadow, who'd reentered the thick brush.

A whistle shrilled, halting both Taylor and Wyatt in their tracks.

"Who was that?" Taylor asked.

A whistle answered, but from the opposite direction.

Another came from the left, then the right.

"Hunters." Wyatt grabbed Taylor's arm. "They're herding us."

Shadow's low growl sounded ahead of them.

Taylor drew out her gun. "Stay close."

Wyatt took a step, but his boot caught on something.

He shifted the beam downward and gasped.

A trip wire.

He shoved Taylor to the right just as a spiked log swung down from the trees, narrowly missing them.

Taylor's sharp inhale revealed her surprise. "They knew we'd come this way."

"Which means they've been watching and were ready for us." Wyatt unleashed his weapon and scanned the area, his flashlight catching an object in the beam. "I see something over there." He pointed before moving carefully around the spiked trap and kneeled in front of the item in question.

Another crumpled piece of paper.

Wyatt didn't wait for Taylor, but flattened it out. A single, messy word was scrawled in crayon.

HƎLP!

Wyatt sucked in a breath. "No!"

Taylor rushed to his side. "What is it?"

He lifted the paper. "This is from Levi. He writes his *e*'s backward."

Voices sounded to the left.

"Turn off your light," Wyatt whispered. "They're here."

She obeyed.

Flashlight beams cut through the trees, heading in their direction.

A child's scream pierced through the storm.

"Levi!" His son's cry sent Wyatt's heartbeat racing, threatening to explode out of his chest.

The hunters had found Levi before Wyatt could.

FOUR

Thunder boomed, adding to Wyatt's already amplified panic levels and thrusting him into a full-fledged state of terror, immobilizing him. *Move! Now!* His leaden legs wouldn't listen to his brain's silent command. Another scream propelled him into action. His son needed him. Wyatt whipped out his Glock, raising his light and gun in one swift motion in the trajectory of his son's cry.

A flash of camouflage illuminated in the beam of light between the trees. A masked suspect carried Wyatt's son over his shoulder.

Levi looked in Wyatt's direction, his eyes full of terror. "Papa, help me!" His tiny arm stretched out to his father, a plea for aid.

But too far out of Wyatt's grasp.

"Taylor, over there!" Wyatt pointed. "He's got Levi."

Gunfire erupted from both sides of Wyatt's and Taylor's positions. The hunters had formed a deadly circle of protection for their leader, helping him to escape with Levi.

Ridge tilted his head and mimed shooting Wyatt with his free hand before dashing off with Levi.

Wyatt hitched in a breath and hesitated. Something about his stance felt familiar, but why? Time seemed to freeze, similar to his son's favorite superhero movies—and once again, Wyatt struggled to move. Struggled to remember where he'd seen Levi's abductor before.

Bullets kicked up dust and leaves at Wyatt's feet, causing him to stumble backward as Ridge ducked between the trees, disappearing with Levi.

No!

Somewhere in the distance, a dog barked and a woman's voice yelled for him to move, but his feet wouldn't obey.

He failed his son. Failed his wife by not saving Levi.

And failed himself for not being able to do the one thing he had promised himself since her death.

Protect their son.

More shots echoed with the thunder, intermixing with the pouring rain and drenching him within seconds.

A firm hand latched on to his arm, yanking him to the ground and bulldozing him out of his thoughts of failure.

"Wyatt, snap out of it and protect yourself!" Taylor fired shots to the left. "Shadow, protect!"

The dog barked ferociously and barreled through the tree line toward where Ridge had disappeared.

"We have to follow. Pull yourself together to save your son." Taylor's voice held a forceful but gentle command. "Please."

She was right. His frozen state of shock wouldn't help Levi. *Keep your eyes in nature...*

Suddenly, his father's words thudded into Wyatt's mind. He had to use his knowledge of this park against Ridge in order to find his son. "I'm sorry. Fear immobilized me, but I'm good. We have to figure out where they would take him."

Taylor raised her weapon in multiple directions. "I think the shooters are gone. They were only creating a diversion to take Levi." She stowed her weapon and pressed her radio button, requesting assistance at their location.

Shadow returned, gave a sharp bark, then turned and zipped back the way he'd come.

"What's he doing?" Wyatt stood and pivoted in a one-eighty circle to get his bearings.

"He's caught a scent." Taylor brought out her gun and followed her dog.

Wyatt chased after them, shaking off his earlier thoughts of failure. He would save his son if it was the last thing he did.

Taylor and Wyatt found Shadow digging under a cluster of pines moments later.

"He's found something." Dread tightened Wyatt's chest. *Please, God, help it not be Levi.* Wyatt searched in all directions for suspects before approaching the dog.

Shadow continued to paw at a pile of leaves and dirt.

Taylor holstered her gun and squatted. "What is it, boy?"

The K-9 barked and sat, exposing his find.

Levi's dark brown hoodie.

Wyatt dropped to his knees. "No!"

Now his son was without a jacket in a pounding thunderstorm.

Tears burned behind Wyatt's eyes, but he balled his fists, redirecting the rising horror surging inside him.

Taylor squeezed Wyatt's shoulder. "He's smart and leaving us clues."

Wyatt swallowed his threatening emotions and pushed himself upright. "But this is the opposite direction of where they went. Could they have traveled that quickly in—"

Shadow barked, interrupting Wyatt's question. The K-9 dashed into the trees.

"He's caught another scent." Taylor ran after her dog.

Wyatt snatched his son's hoodie. Levi would need his jacket for warmth from the chilling rain once they found him.

And they *would* find him.

Resolve locked Wyatt's shoulders as he charged after the duo.

Wyatt took off his cowboy hat and wiped the rain from his forehead moments later. "What did Shadow find?"

Taylor placed her hands on her hips. "No idea, but we're back where we started. Odd. Shadow appears to be confused." She motioned at her dog.

He sniffed the foliage, then trotted back to the path before pivoting and returning to the clump of bushes.

Realization punched Wyatt in the gut and he shoved his hat back on. "They're moving Levi in loops."

"Sending us in circles to ensure we don't follow them." She puffed out a sigh. "We have to outsmart them. You know this park better than anyone. Where would they go?"

An idea formed, and Wyatt waggled his fingers at Taylor. "Can you show me Levi's drawing again?"

She dug into her pocket and brought the paper out, unfolding it.

Wyatt leaned over her shoulder and analyzed his son's drawing. A memory rose. "Wait." He pointed to the bridge. "About four years ago, when I was a rookie, I stumbled across someone smuggling crates of weapons across the old rusted out bridge at Kesbush Gorge. It's a faster route out of the park, so that's why they chose it."

"They? Did you catch the smugglers?"

"No. They abandoned the few crates we found and park workers tore down the bridge. It was too dangerous, but they labeled it the red bridge." He gritted his teeth. "I can't believe I didn't remember that before."

"Don't beat yourself up. You've had lots on your mind." Her face softened, revealing the kindness he remembered from their short dating days.

Before she broke his heart.

Don't go there. Now isn't the time. "Levi must have heard them talking about it. It has to be where they're headed."

"Where is it?"

"In the opposite direction of here. That's why they were sending us in circles. It wasn't Levi giving us breadcrumbs this time, it was Ridge and his hunters." Wyatt's pulse spiked as anger at himself slammed into him like a freight train. "And I fell for it."

"Don't take all the ownership on you. They fooled both myself and Shadow." She gestured toward her K-9. "And that's tough to do. These guys are smart." She tucked the drawing away. "But you're smarter, Wyatt Hoyt. Let's use your knowledge of the park against them."

His gaze locked on to hers, analyzing her beautiful face. "You always were a good encourager."

"Well, your father didn't only teach Levi, he taught you." She grinned.

Wyatt tore his eyes away from her captivating smile that always was his undoing.

And still is.

He cleared his throat to silence the stir of old feelings. Their connection two years ago had caught him totally off guard. He never fell so quickly for a woman—even Lisa. Oh, he loved his wife with all his heart—still did—but their relationship had a rocky start because of Wyatt's cocky attitude. Lisa eventually wore down his tough exterior and made him see how he had masked his insecurities with arrogant actions. She had made him a better man.

And he would always be grateful for her guidance, but something woke in him the second he met Taylor. At least for him.

Even so, right now wasn't the time to ponder that. She wasn't interested. Plus, he wouldn't risk her breaking his heart again.

And he had to find his son.

He wouldn't lose the most important thing in his life.

Levi Kyle Hoyt.

Taylor struggled to avert her gaze from the handsome conservation officer's face as a question rose in her mind. What was he thinking? The way his stare burrowed made her suspect it was something other than the situation at hand. *Step away.* The inner warning tore her eyes from him and she bent over, ruffling Shadow's fur. Anything to break the awkward silence. She pushed her attraction deep from the depths of her being. She couldn't or wouldn't go there. Taylor dug her nails into her palms until they ached. *So be it.* The pain was nothing like the pain of letting him go years ago.

No, she wouldn't let herself fall again.

She straightened. "How far is this red bridge?"

"Approximately an hour's hike." Wyatt checked his watch. "I guess they have about a twenty-minute head start with all of their false clues. It's getting late and Levi is probably frantic."

"Let's get going, then. Which way?"

He gestured to the right. "Follow me. I know a shortcut." He didn't wait, but hurried through the brush.

"I guessed you would. Shadow, come."

The dog hopped up onto all fours, ready to work.

Taylor updated her fellow officers and provided directions on their heading to Kesbush Gorge, warning them to take extreme caution. A boy was caught in the crosshairs of a killer.

And she would not put Levi in harm's way.

She hustled to catch up to Wyatt. "What can you tell me about the smugglers from four years ago?" Taylor not only wanted to pass the time it would take to reach the gorge, but keep Wyatt's thoughts from overtaking and immobilizing him like they had earlier. "That was before we met."

"Yes, and a few weeks before Lisa's death." He paused, as if gathering his thoughts and memories. "I was six months into my role here and struggling."

"How? You always seemed confident in your conservation officer's duties to me."

"Not back then. I had failed to ticket some hunters who gave me a sob story about how they left their license in their truck. I gave them the benefit of the doubt and only warned them to do better next time, but Cam caught up with them later and discovered they lied."

"Let me guess. He wrote you up." She could relate. Another female constable had done the same to her when she lost a suspect. All because the woman was jealous of how their leader took Taylor under his wing.

"Yep, and he still brings that up to this day. He's our supervisor's favorite, and he reminds the rest of us almost daily."

He stopped and faced her, rain dripping off his hat's rim. "I've learned a lot since my rookie days, but unfortunately, Cam and I still butt heads. Anyway, I was patrolling and hiked up to the gorge. I heard voices and investigated. I found two men carrying crates across the rusted bridge. They were halfway when they spotted me and hustled to the other side. One dropped a crate."

Wyatt continued on their trek through the trees.

She followed as rain pummeled the region, turning their climb up the mountain into a treacherous hike. One minor slip could send them tumbling.

Wyatt glanced over his shoulder. "That's when I saw the weapons. I radioed it in and followed the duo, but both got away. To make a long story short, police investigated and arrested one smuggler, but the other was never found. That I'm aware of."

"What happened next?"

"The smuggler told police he didn't know the leader but gave them details of their plans, which eventually led to a few more arrests. None of the prisoners claimed to be the leader. The park eventually tore the bridge down to stop any further weapon trafficking and hikers from using the unstable route."

Fork lightning bolts flashed across the sky, illuminating their path and sending shivers down Taylor's back. She shared Levi's hate for thunderstorms, even though her mother had tried to convince Taylor's six-year-old mind that it was simply God bowling.

Thunder rumbled, thrusting Taylor out of the memory. "So essentially, you stopped this ring."

"Well, not just me. Yes, I was the one who stumbled across their illegal activity, but it was a joint effort."

"You don't give yourself enough credit." A thought rose. "Wait, do you think it's possible this is the same ring restarting their efforts to get weapons?"

He stopped and turned to face her. "Perhaps, police only arrested the one smuggler, and he was found hanging in his cell two months later. Apparent suicide."

Taylor grunted. "Doubtful. Someone made it look that way, so he wouldn't rat out the leader."

He tilted his head. "But why this park? There must be better areas to smuggle weapons in."

Taylor pictured Levi's drawing. "What if they're not smuggling in but out?"

"What are you suggesting?"

"Remember Levi's odd-looking bow and arrow? What if this gang is somehow enhancing these weapons in the forest and smuggling them *out* of the park?"

His eyes brightened as if a light bulb went off in his head. "That makes sense. What better place to do it without multiple eyes spying on them? Especially in this neck of the woods. It's dangerous and few hikers venture into the gorge area. Plus, this part of the park is close to the Labrador Sea and the North Atlantic Ocean."

"The perfect place to smuggle. Easy access. They can ship to different locations around the world and make millions. No wonder they're ruthless." Taylor rubbed her chin. "But why were the smugglers back on the trail where Levi and Denise spotted them and not here?"

"Meeting their buyer?" He held up his index finger. "Wait, I noticed that the man they killed seemed to have one leg shorter than the other. I thought it was just the angle he fell, but what if he couldn't handle this rough terrain and demanded they meet on the trail to complete their deal?"

"You have a point." Another thought came to mind, but she'd have to word her assumptions carefully. "I hate to say this, but why kidnap Levi and not remove him from the equation like they had Denise?"

His jaw dropped. "Good question."

Lightning struck nearby, followed seconds later by a boom echoing throughout the woods.

"We must find my son. Now!" Wyatt continued ahead, increasing his pace.

She agreed and sprinted after him. They had to find the boy before this ring smuggled out their weapons, because at that point, Levi would be of no value to them.

He was running out of precious time.

FIVE

Wyatt veered to the left, taking another shortcut, but slowed his pace. The terrain he chose was risky in the best of times, but had grown even more hazardous in the slick conditions, and he would not risk falling. His son's life depended on him reaching the gorge before they did. Wyatt's stomach twisted, a tangled mess of grief and fear knotting inside him like a rope stretched to the snapping point, threatening to overpower him. *Keep it together. Levi needs you.*

Wyatt ignored the battle going on in his mind and took the rugged trail that hugged the cliffs of the Kesbush Gorge. "Stay close. This path is dangerous at the best of times."

"Will do." Taylor commanded Shadow to heel. The dog hovered close to her side in obedience.

Good. Wyatt had to ensure they were safe, too, as he wouldn't let anything happen to them. Not when they were here to save Levi's life.

The group emerged into a clearing and stopped steps away from the cliff's edge.

Wyatt motioned to the right. "This will get us to the 'red bridge' quicker." He air-quoted *red bridge*.

Taylor's gaze shifted to the rocky steep trail and her expression morphed into one of terror.

Not that he blamed her. This path was not for the faint of heart…and it was about to get worse.

Much worse.

A question came to his mind. "Taylor, are you scared of heights?"

She bit her lip and nodded.

Wyatt stopped and reached for her hand, squeezing. "Stay close. I won't let anything happen to you."

He studied the skies again, thankful the storm had subsided for now. He didn't relish the thought of having to take the cliff wall path in the dark. They had to hurry. *God, if You're listening, give us steady steps.*

Taylor tugged on his hand. "Can we take a quick second to stop and pray?"

"Of course. Go ahead." Anything to help with their precarious predicament, even prayers to an unseen God.

She bowed her head. "Lord, we ask You to stop the storm and give us careful footing as we take this treacherous path. Help us get to Levi and save him. In Jesus's name, Amen."

"Amen." He released her hand. "Let's go. Single file from here."

The trio continued on their trek through the unpredictable terrain. Five minutes later, they reached the spot where the bridge had once been. Wyatt stopped when he discovered what the smuggler had obviously constructed to get their goods across the gorge.

A pulley system anchored from the cliff's wall over to the other side.

"Wait, this is how they're getting the weapons across?" Taylor squatted and examined the system.

They had used a portion of the rusted bridge and mounted the wheel to the side, extending the thick steel rope through a large metal wire cage.

Wyatt would've been impressed by their ingenuity if they were using their powers for good and not evil.

"Interesting. What I want to know is how they constructed this without others either seeing or hearing them." Wyatt wiped his forehead.

"Didn't you say no one normally comes to this region?"

"Yes, but I wonder how long this has been here?"

Taylor fingered the device. "The rope and basket are still shiny, so it's been recent. When was the last time you were here?"

"Mid-fall before winter took over."

Voices sounded below.

Wyatt bristled and peered over the edge.

Two men were placing Levi into a boat above the rapids.

"No!" He pointed. "They beat us and are taking Levi across this dangerous river. We have to stop them." He gestured to the jagged rock narrow path. "I've taken the route before, so step where I step, but hug the wall." He braced himself for her reaction.

She blinked rapidly, the color draining from her face. "The wall?"

"We must take the steep path that hugs the cliff's wall and empties below at the riverbank." He hated the terror twisting her pretty face. "I'm sorry, Taylor. It's the only way to get to Levi and save him. I can go alone. I don't want to put you and Shadow at risk."

She crumpled to the rocky ground. Shadow whined and licked her face, obviously sensing his handler's emotions.

He squatted in front of her. "Stay here and radio for help."

Another rumble echoed throughout the mountain region.

Wyatt examined the sky. The clouds had deepened to a sinister shade of gray, churning fast and heavy, as if warning anyone in their path of what was heading their way. Not good.

He stood. "I have to go before it gets darker. There's no way I'd make it down once those clouds unleash their wrath. Hail on a cliff is never a good thing. We're running out of time."

She breathed in an audible breath and released it slowly before standing. "I'm coming. I can't go back because I'd get lost and not trusting a fellow partner's gut didn't turn out so good for me before."

"What do you mean?" Curiosity gnawed at Wyatt like termites on fresh wood.

"We can talk about it later. If you're right—" she gestured toward the clouds before continuing "—it's time to move."

"As my mom always says, 'God's got us' and I have to believe that right now." Although, why didn't God save Kyle, Lisa or Denise? *Why did You let them die?*

Another rumble tore Wyatt from his thoughts. "Time to move." God would have to wait and Wyatt only hoped that He listened to Taylor's earlier prayer. "Remember, step where I step."

"Got it." She turned to Shadow. "Heel."

The dog inched closer to his handler.

The trio continued on the path. Gushing water sounded beneath their location, but Wyatt refused to look over the edge. He knew what lay below.

Rapids.

The only thing going for them right now was the fact that they were out of the darkened forest and in the light.

But that light would soon extinguish with the sun's descent, catapulting their dangerous situation into one Wyatt refused to contemplate.

Taylor halted. "Are those rapids I hear? I don't want to look down."

"I'm not gonna lie. This river is dangerous." He paused. "Yes, fast-moving water is directly below us, but where we're going, the rapids aren't nearly as bad. Stay strong. It's about to get trickier."

He didn't miss her sharp intake of breath.

For Levi's sake, he had to leave Taylor's fear with God. *Mom, I need you on your knees right about now.*

Taylor inched closer and looked down. "We'll never make it."

Wyatt latched on to her wrists. "My son doesn't have time for second guesses. We have to keep moving, but let's leave our backpacks here. We'll hide them since the approaching trail doesn't allow for extras." He removed his pack and stuffed it between two rocks concealed by bushes.

"Understood. I'm calling in our location. We should get a decent signal here. Hopefully." She hit her radio button and gave details on their position, requesting backup. She wiggled out of her pack's straps and placed it beside Wyatt's.

"They'll never get here on time and we don't know for sure that your message went through." Wyatt slapped his hat back on his head. "I'm going."

Lightning flashed as the clouds unleashed a downpour. Not good, but they didn't have a choice.

Move, or let Levi be taken.

"Grab onto anything you can on the cliff's wall." Wyatt read the alarm on her tortured face. "Baby steps."

Shadow barked as if in agreement.

She nodded, her expression morphing into courageous determination.

"Stay close." Wyatt shuffled forward, being careful where he stepped, as he leaned against the cliff.

The group crept along the narrow ledge, their backs pressed tightly to the jagged rock wall. Every step toward the ravine had to remain sure and steady. The only sound booming through their tight space was the roar of the rushing water below.

Halfway down, bullets pinged off rocks ahead of Wyatt. He froze. The hunters spotted them.

"Keep going, Wyatt! We stop and we give them an easy target." Taylor's command propelled him onward.

"Don't shoot back. Levi is somewhere down there."

Another bullet pinged off the cliff wall above them.

Wyatt hustled as fast as he could through the pouring rain, his soggy hiking boots pounding against the slick rocky trail.

The closer they got, the more the spray of bullets pummeled them.

The hunters didn't plan for them to reach the bottom without a fight.

Behind him, Shadow snarled.

Another bullet ricocheted off the rocks at Wyatt's feet.

"They're not trying to kill us but stall us from getting to Levi. Keep moving. We're almost there."

A gunshot cut through the air as searing pain pierced Wyatt's arm. He staggered to a stop, a chilling thought weighing him down.

He was wrong. The hunters weren't targeting them anymore, but trying to eliminate them.

Taylor's gaze flew to his arm. "You're bleeding."

He gripped the wound. "It's only a graze. We have to jump. It's the only way."

Her eyes widened. "Are you kidding me? We're almost there."

"The rapids aren't as strong here. Do you trust me?"

She bit her lip. "Yes." She turned to the shepherd. "Shadow, jump."

"On the count of three. Once you submerge, grab onto anything you can." He hesitated. "One."

Another bullet sprayed dirt at their feet.

"Two."

Levi's cry circled throughout the canyon like a boomerang. It was now or never.

"Three." Wyatt drew in a deep breath.

And jumped.

God, help us! Rain intermixed with hail stung Taylor's face as she plummeted toward the river. The wind cemented her wet hair across her face, blocking her view of the water below. That was probably a good thing. She prayed God would keep Shadow safe, but she knew how strong of a swimmer he was. He was a search and rescue dog, after all.

She, on the other hand, wasn't as strong.

The drop lasted seconds, but felt like an eternity. Time had stilled as they plummeted, air ripped from her lungs as her ears rang with the rush of blood. Her feet crashed into the icy water, swallowing her whole and sending jolts through her nerves. Disorientated from the cold, she fought her way to the top, arms flailing against the strong current until she finally burst through the surface. She snatched in a breath before trying to get her bearings.

Taylor circled in the churning water until she spotted Wyatt swimming toward the shore. Even against the current and his injury, the man's strength amazed her. But she realized it wasn't only his strength driving him forward. It was the weight of what he stood to lose.

His son's life.

She kicked hard to reach the shore—then, without warning, a tornado of rushing water dragged her under. Her survival instincts increased her adrenaline, and she broke back to the surface.

Taylor swam toward Wyatt using all her strength. As she neared the riverbank, she caught a glimpse of her partner.

Perched on a rock by the shore, a soggy ball of fur gave a vigorous shake, releasing droplets of water off his soaked coat.

Thank You, Lord, for saving them both.

Another wave of strong current fought to take Taylor downstream. She flailed her arms and yelled, kicking her weak legs, but she was sucked under. Again.

A muffled splash like a shock wave told her Shadow had jumped back into the river to save her. Moments later, she jolted upward as the shepherd clamped onto her coat's collar, holding her in a firm grip.

He dragged her back to the surface.

She gulped in a breath and kicked to help her powerful dog pull her to the shore.

Two hands reached into the water and lugged her the rest of the way. "I've got you," Wyatt said. "Good boy, Shadow."

Together, the trio climbed over the rocks and long weeds, crawling up onto the riverbank.

Shadow growled seconds before Taylor sensed another presence.

"Hold it right there." The masked man held a rifle to their heads.

However, he underestimated the dog to his right.

"Get 'em!" Taylor prayed her low but intense command would work.

Shadow launched into the air and latched onto the man's arm, knocking the rifle to the ground.

Taylor scrambled the rest of the way onto the shore and snatched the weapon before the man could react. She aimed it at him. "Stand down."

"Get this beast off me."

"Call him that again and I'll unleash him fully on you." Not that Taylor would do that to an unarmed suspect, but if the man threatened their lives, she wouldn't hesitate.

He cursed. "Fine. I surrender."

"Shadow, out," Taylor commanded.

The dog released him and Wyatt hurried to the man's side, wrenching him upright. "Where is my son?"

"Don't know what you're talking about." He clamped his lips shut.

The hunter wasn't about to make it easy for them.

"Don't believe you." Wyatt whipped off the man's mask. "Who do you work for?"

"What makes you think I'm not the boss?"

Taylor guffawed and inched closer. "Because Ridge wouldn't have been so careless."

He flinched.

Gotcha.

"Give up the boy's location and maybe we'll try to cut a deal." Taylor doubted that would happen, but she wasn't about to share her thought.

"He'll kill me if he knew I snitched on him. He's done it before. His tentacles reach within the police department and prisons."

Fear laced the hunter's voice, reminding Taylor of what Wyatt had shared earlier about the last smuggler imprisoned that had supposedly hung himself. Was it possible that Ridge was the same smuggler Wyatt had stopped years ago?

Taylor lowered the rifle slightly to signify an olive branch. She had to get on this man's good side. "We will get you protection. Tell us where Levi is."

"I got a family, man."

"So do I. That boy is my son!" Wyatt's grip on the hunter tightened.

Shadow growled.

"Okay, let's stay calm." With her right hand, Taylor unhooked her cuffs and passed them to Wyatt. "Secure him to a tree."

Wyatt shoved the suspect over to a birch and made him sit on the ground. He wrapped his arms around the skinny trunk and cuffed him. "There. He's not going anywhere. Now talk."

"Ridge has your boy secured to a tree down that way." He nodded toward the area opposite of where the ring had constructed the new pulley system across the gorge. "Getting him ready to transport."

"Transport where?" Wyatt asked.

The man shrugged. "We're never told the destination, but he mentioned the boy would get him extra money."

Wyatt hissed in a ragged breath. "We have to rescue him, Taylor."

She read the frantic level in his voice, but Taylor had to find out how many hunters surrounded his son. She wouldn't walk into a trap. "How many are guarding Levi?" She raised the rifle again. "And don't lie to me."

"Two, but you better hurry if you want to see the boy before Ridge ships him out."

"Let's go, Taylor." Wyatt sprinted into the trees.

"Hold up. We need a plan." She glanced at her dog. "Shadow, come."

"What about me?" the man asked.

"Don't worry. We'll send the police to your location."

"But it's getting late and there are animals in these parts."

"Right now, the animals are the least of your worries." Taylor ignored the man's obvious fear and headed into the forest with Shadow at her heels.

She caught up to Wyatt. "Wait. Let me check your arm."

He halted in his tracks. "It's fine. A simple nick." He shifted positions, revealing his upper arm.

She quickly examined the wound as best she could through his torn jacket. "Doesn't appear to be too deep. Your coat must have taken the brunt of the bullet as it grazed you. Can you hold a rifle steady?"

"Of course. I helped Shadow drag you out of the water, didn't I?"

"Yes, but our adrenaline helped. We—"

"Bossman said to get the boy ready," a raspy voice said ahead of them.

Taylor stilled and inspected the forest. Glimpses of two hunters in camouflage flashed through the trees. She gestured toward them and handed Wyatt the rifle. "You secure the one on the right. Restrain them so they can't call any other hunters into the area."

"What are you going to do?"

"Shadow and I will subdue the other one." She squatted in front of her K-9. "Boy, I'm so glad you're okay. I'm relying on you." She hugged him before releasing her partner. "Shadow, silent."

The dog lifted his snout and snuggled into her.

She stood and faced Wyatt head-on. "We have to be quick. Do you still make that funny birdcall you did when we first met?"

"Yes."

"Okay, when you get close to the hunter, do your call. That will tell me to move. Go!"

"Copy." He took off to the right.

"Shadow, protect!" Taylor darted from tree to tree until she spotted Levi sitting on the ground tied to an aspen, a guard towering over him.

To her right, a birdcall shrilled through the forest. Her sign to act. "Shadow, get 'em!"

The dog zipped through the forest and pounced onto the unsuspecting hunter, hauling him to the ground.

The man swore and cried out.

Taylor punched the man square in the face.

He collapsed to the ground, out cold.

Taylor scurried over to Levi and untied him. "Let's go, Levi."

"Daddy?"

"He's coming." Taylor used the rope to secure the hunter.

"I'm right here, son." Wyatt handed the rifle to Taylor and bounded to his son's side. He dropped to his knees, bringing Levi into his arms. "Daddy's got you."

Levi wrapped his little arms around Wyatt's neck and clung tightly.

Shadow growled, warning them of further danger.

Taylor gripped the rifle tighter, bracing herself for a fight.

Wyatt lifted Levi and stood. "Taylor, time to move. Someone's coming."

"But we have to catch Ridge."

"Not with my son's life at stake. We don't know how many more hunters are out here. We're probably outnumbered."

"You're right, but we can't go up the cliff's trail. It's too dangerous."

"Agreed. We'll have to go around. It's longer, but safer. Come on." Wyatt didn't wait, but slipped into the forest.

Taylor commanded Shadow to protect and follow, a question lingering in her mind.

How many hunters patrolled this part of the remote wilderness?

SIX

Wyatt held his son in a vise grip as he blasted as silently as he could through the forest, not wanting to attract further attention to any hunters, especially the ruthless Ridge. Wyatt sidestepped a protruding cluster of bushes but caught sight of a half-buried crate. Could this be some of the gang's weapons? He couldn't think of that right now. He'd send police officers back to this location to retrieve the crate, along with the hunters they secured. Right now, he had one thing on his mind.

Get Levi out of the forest and to safety. He would not risk his son's life. He'd been through enough.

The rain continued to hammer the region after ninety minutes of hiking through the rugged paths of Teragoose National Park, but the thunder and lightning had subsided. Darkness now blanketed the region and Wyatt relied on Taylor's light to illuminate their path as well as her K-9's keen sense.

Almost there. *You can do this.*

His injured arm throbbed and the added weight of carrying Levi only increased his pain level, but Wyatt forged ahead with determination as he marshaled strength into his weary body.

"How much farther to the park station?" Taylor's question broke the silence.

Thankfully, they hadn't encountered any more hunters, and the forest had stilled as if it once again held its peacefulness to all who entered. The eerie feeling subsided, and the wilderness went to sleep even though a smuggling ring had taken up residence within its forest.

"I estimate another thirty minutes. Let's take a five-minute break. Can you try your radio again?" Wyatt set Levi on a large rock. "You good to stay here, bud?" He squatted in front of his boy.

"Yes, Papa."

Even after everything the five-year-old had been through today, he still appeared in good spirits.

Which was more than he could say for himself. He stood and turned to Taylor. "Anything?"

She shook the radio. "Nope, still waterlogged. I'm afraid it's toast." She addressed her K-9 and gestured toward Levi. "Shadow, protect."

The dog trotted to Levi's side. Levi snuggled into him, wrapping his tiny arms around Shadow's neck. "I love you, Shadow."

The sight both warmed Wyatt and sent him back two years when the pair had snuggled in front of the fireplace at Wyatt's ranch. They became friends within minutes of meeting.

Wyatt bit the inside of his mouth to squash the image. He couldn't go there. For Levi's sake and his own. He wasn't sure that either of them would survive another heartbreak.

"I can't believe how resilient my son is." Wyatt leaned closer to Taylor, massaging his throbbing arm. "He's stronger than his father."

"I highly doubt that. Do you want me to carry him for a bit?"

"No." His response came a little too quickly. He didn't miss her lips purse, even in the darkness. "Sorry. I'm just a little reluctant to let go." Half-truth. What he really didn't want was his son to get attached to the woman in front of him.

Who knew how long she'd be in their lives this time around and Wyatt wasn't about to risk his son's little heart.

"I understand." She shone the light on her watch. "It's now nine thirty, and it's been a long day. Shall we keep moving?"

"Yes." Wyatt plodded over to his son and kneeled in front of him. "Ready to go home, Levi?"

"Yes, Papa!" Levi reached out and touched Wyatt's head. "Cowboy hat?"

Wyatt grimaced. His favorite cowboy hat was probably floating out in the Labrador Sea by now. He hated to lose the hat Lisa had given him on their last Christmas together, but he couldn't wallow in self-pity. His son was safe and Wyatt's plummet into the Kesbush River had been necessary to get to him.

So be it.

Wyatt lifted Levi again and winced silently from the pain shooting throughout his arm. "Papa lost it, but I have more."

Lots more. His cowboy hat fetish had always made Lisa laugh when he bought another one. And why Field had nicknamed Wyatt "cowboy."

"Time to go home, son."

"Shadow and Taylor, too?" Levi's innocent question silenced everything and everyone in the forest.

Except for Taylor's sharp inhale.

Levi snuggled into Wyatt's hold and laid his head on his shoulder. Within moments he fell asleep, not waiting for any response to his question.

Wyatt cleared his throat. "Shall we?"

He slugged up the steps of Teragoose National Park's station thirty-five minutes later. He ushered strength into his legs, but the weight of carrying his son was taking its toll on his weary limbs.

"Let me get the door." Taylor sidestepped him and thrust open the glass door.

Warmth from the room greeted Wyatt like a warm blanket on a frigid winter day. Even in June, the temps in the mountains were cold and they had also taken a swim in an icy pool, which only added to his chilled bones.

"There you are." Park Warden Huxley Price tipped his head toward the two constables hovering in the background. "We've all been trying to reach you on your radios."

"Thanks, Hux. I'm afraid we took an unplanned dip in the Kesbush River." Wyatt headed to the couch in the visitors' area and laid his son down, relief filling his arms.

Supervisor Xavier Bain stomped toward them, with Cam Field not far behind.

Great, between the two of them, Wyatt was in for an earful, and he wasn't in the mood for their joint reprimand.

Wyatt raised both arms to block them, but Taylor stepped in front of him.

"Guys, we're tired and Wyatt needs a paramedic along with his son, Levi. Wyatt took a graze from a bullet and it requires attention." Taylor motioned toward her dog. "And Shadow is probably parched. It's been a long day."

"I'll get your dog something." Hux disappeared into the station's lunchroom.

Bain turned to Field. "Call for EMS while I find out what happened."

Field tipped his chin and headed to the welcome desk.

Bain faced Taylor. "Now, if you don't mind. I would like to hear what happened from my employee, but first, who are you?"

Wyatt shifted his stance. "Constable Taylor Grant and her K-9 Shadow. She helped me find my son, sir. If it wasn't for them, I'd still be out in that wilderness."

Hux returned holding a bowl of water and some beef jerky, passing it to Taylor. "Here you go."

"Thank you." Taylor kneeled and placed the bowl on the floor, holding out the treat to Shadow. "No seasonings, boy. I promise. You deserve this for all your hard work today."

Hux placed his hands on his hips. "Now, tell us what happened in my park."

Field reappeared. "EMS is on their way."

Wyatt and Taylor spent the next ten minutes explaining what events occurred in the park, including the reemergence of the weapon smuggling ring, and the new pulley system at the Kesbush Gorge.

Hux's jaw dropped. "How in the world did they do that with no one knowing?"

Of the three men, Hux had always been the friendliest to Wyatt. They were both in their early thirties and from a large family, so they had hit it off instantly when they met.

"I asked the same thing, Hux. I'm guessing they constructed it after hunting season officially ended and most visitors had vacated the park, especially that dangerous region." Wyatt rubbed his temples, warding off the emerging headache. Not that it surprised him with all the stress of the day and lack of food. Right now, all he wanted to do was take his son home.

"Hoyt, you look terrible," Bain said. "Take tomorrow off. I'll get Cam to cover you."

"Thanks, sir." Wyatt could certainly use a good night's sleep.

"Get your report to me tomorrow, though. I gotta run. Glad you're okay." Bain exited the building as two paramedics rushed through the doors.

After a thorough examination, the paramedics agreed with Taylor's assessment of Wyatt's wound. His jacket had blocked most of the bullet's graze and the cut wasn't deep. They cleaned the area and bandaged him after they had checked Levi for injuries. He had passed with flying colors.

Levi now sat on the couch eating a granola bar.

"Taylor, can you update the constables on the exact location of where we left the restrained hunters?" He motioned toward Levi. "Then I'd like to get him home to bed."

"Of course. Be right back." Taylor trudged toward the two constables who waited patiently for her report.

"Hux, I need a favor and I hate to ask this." Wyatt cringed at what he required his friend to do. "I don't trust anyone else."

"Anything for you, bro." Hux leaned closer. "I hate how Cam treats you. What is it?"

Wyatt told him how they had to abandon their backpacks and explained where. "Can you retrieve them for us first thing in the morning? I know that's a huge ask. It's quite a distance."

Hux patted his stomach. "I need the exercise. I'll get it and bring it to your ranch. That okay?"

Wyatt slapped his friend on the back. "I owe you big-time."

"Like I said, anything for you. After all, you saved my behind a month ago when you scared that bear out of my path. Now go. You look terrible and need sleep."

Wyatt chuckled and picked up his tired son.

Ten minutes later, Taylor turned onto the highway that would take them to Wyatt's ranch.

"I appreciate you driving us. I realize Cam offered, but I know he'd drill me all the way home." *Besides, even after a terrifying day, you're better to look at than him.* Did he really just think that? Thankfully, he kept the thought to himself. Wyatt stole a peek at his son in the back seat. "Levi is out like a light."

"He's exhausted and you're very welcome. Yeah, that Cam seems annoying."

"You don't know the half of it. He—"

A cell phone sitting in a holder on her console rang.

"Wait, I thought your phone was ruined?"

"Only my work cell phone. That's my personal one and my leader is calling. I have to take this."

"Of course."

Taylor hit the button. "Sergeant Mitchell, I'm here with Conservation Officer Wyatt Hoyt. What do you have for us?"

"Couple things. First, an update on the airstrip. No suspicious activity there, but from what you told the others, I'm guessing they smuggle using mostly ships."

"Possibly, but we still should monitor the airstrip," Taylor said. "They probably ship by land, sea and air."

"Agreed. Constables are on their way to arrest those hunters. Okay, the other thing isn't good." His tone held concern.

Wyatt sat straighter in his seat, bracing for whatever news the sergeant would share.

"What is it, sir?"

"Taylor, the station received a threat against you, Levi and Wyatt. They seemed to think you have something of theirs and they want it back."

Wyatt fumed. "Sir, did they say what it was?"

"No, just that they'd kill you if you didn't return their property." A hissed breath sailed through the phone. "Taylor, I don't like the bull's-eye they've put on all your backs. Please lie low for a few days and protect the boy."

Wyatt observed Taylor's profile.

She chewed on her lip.

A habit he remembered from two years ago. She was nervous.

"You can stay with us. We have plenty of room." Wait, had he just offered to let her back into their lives when earlier he only wanted her out?

He was definitely tired.

Taylor's grip strangled the steering wheel as thoughts of being in close proximity to the two males in her cruiser sent jabs of both panic and comfort throughout her entire body. If the last twelve hours had proved anything, it was that she was in big trouble. Being around these two had pummeled her backward two years to the time she had fallen—for both.

And it wouldn't be long before she fell again.

"Taylor? That okay?" Wyatt's questions brought her back into her vehicle.

Shadow woofed like he agreed.

Ugh! She was outnumbered. "Fine. That should work. Your ranch is off the beaten path and secluded."

"Good, it's settled, then," Sergeant Mitchell said.

She'd forgotten in that brief lapse of panic that he was still on the line. "Sir, can you maybe have cruisers patrol that area as well?"

"I will. Has Levi said anything more than what the officers told me on the phone?"

Taylor noted Levi was still fast asleep in the back seat. No way they'd be getting any information out of him tonight. "I suggest we talk to him tomorrow." She flipped her gaze to Wyatt's. "Sound good?"

His fingers noticeably tightened on the armrest.

"I can guess what you're thinking, Wyatt. He's been through a lot." She reached over and squeezed his hand. "We'll ensure he gets a good sleep and breakfast before we bring anything up. I promise."

"Wyatt, I understand your concern," Mitchell said. "But we must get ahead of this gang. If what you think is true, and this Ridge is the one you stopped four years ago, he's probably regrouped and is even more dangerous after having that long to plan. And—" he paused before continuing "—not only your lives are at stake. If these modified, dangerous weapons get into the wrong hands, more lives will be at risk."

"I understand. Just let me do the talking. I know my son the best." Wyatt drew his hand away from Taylor's.

Taylor didn't miss his hidden insinuation. She had to remain in the background. Levi had only been three when she and Wyatt dated. "Understood." Even though she did, his implication still pierced her heart.

Not that she blamed him. She had broken his.

"Okay, it's settled," her sergeant said. "Oh, Dr. Oke told me she should have an identification on the deceased male you found in the woods soon. I'll update you when I hear."

"Thank you, sir." Maybe once they found out the male's identity, it would lead the team to Ridge and his hunters.

Hopefully.

"Okay, I'll say night now. Taylor, promise me you'll stay alert and safe."

"I will, and we have the best of the best protecting us." She adjusted the mirror and stole a glimpse of the furry protector sleeping in his cage. Yes, indeed. "Night, sir." She punched off the call.

"Look, I realize this may be difficult for both of us because of our past." Wyatt's whispered words filled the front seats. "But for my son's sake, can we leave the past where it belongs?"

Was that really possible? Seeing him again today had only brought that past to the forefront. But Wyatt was right.

She'd do as he asked. Levi's life depended on her doing her job.

"Agreed." She inhaled. Exhaled. "Wait, I need clothes, but my place is in the opposite direction."

"My sister Iris visits me often to practice her smoke jumper techniques and has left clothes at my place. You're about the same size. I'm sure she wouldn't mind."

"Thanks. Just thought of something else. You and I both need new phones. That dip in the rapids destroyed ours." Taylor hit her signal light and veered off at the next ramp. "I have to grab some food for Shadow and toiletries for me. I'll text Bryan and ask him to look into getting us phones and a new radio for me."

"Bryan? You and Sergeant Mitchell close?"

Oops. She let his first name slip. She had promised him she'd only call him Bryan when they weren't around others. "Yes. He was my very first boss and took me under his wing when he found out about how my dad walked out on Mom and me. Even after returning from Nova Scotia, he's still here. He and his wife, Joan, have me over for Sunday brunch after church every week."

"You go to church?" He gazed out his passenger window.

"God still a sore spot for you?" She remembered how he'd confessed when they'd dated that he didn't believe like his parents, but he never explained why. Just shut the conversation down, so she let it slide since she wasn't planning on falling for him.

She silently huffed. Like that went well.

"Yep, much to my mom's dismay. It's not that I don't believe in God. I just don't understand why He allows things."

"I think that's a question all Christians have, Wyatt. I certainly do. But I know one thing." She gathered her words carefully so she wouldn't scare him away. "No matter what storms life brings us, He's always with us. Even when we can't feel His presence."

"I wish I could trust that." His words were barely a whisper.

God, show him it's true.

Taylor drove into the store's sparse lot and parked close to the entrance. "I'll be right back." She ensured no one had followed her and that the area was secure before climbing out of her vehicle and hustling inside.

After gathering food and supplies, Taylor pulled through Wyatt's ranch gate twenty minutes later and drove down Wyatt's long laneway, parking in front of his modest log ranch. She cut the engine. "Let's get Levi inside, so you can put him to bed."

Even though it was late, Taylor put the teakettle on while Wyatt tended to his son. She was still wired from the multiple rushes of adrenaline that had flowed through her body all day. Wyatt had told her he'd put some of Iris's clothes in the guest room for her. She had gathered her police-issued laptop and her phone, setting them on the counter before feeding Shadow. Now it was time for a good cup of the lavender-chamomile tea she had purchased at the store. It was her favorite go-to tea for relaxation.

And she had a feeling she'd need it after today and being here at Wyatt's ranch. She breathed in the fresh citrus scent she remembered from two years ago, the aroma calming her frayed nerves.

Her cell phone dinged a text message, interrupting her deep breathing. Probably her sergeant. She reached across the counter and swiped the screen to bring it to life, peering closer.

Don't think you can hide that boy for long. Give back what you took or you all die. R

Taylor sucked in a breath.

Great. No amount of citrus or lavender tea would settle her nerves now.

SEVEN

Wyatt padded into the kitchen in his sock feet after settling Levi in his bed and promising him chocolate chip pancakes for breakfast. Wyatt smiled as he pictured his son's peaceful face when he fell asleep after Wyatt read the first line of Levi's favorite bedtime story. If only Wyatt felt that same peace right now. Someone was after his son, and it was Wyatt's job to protect him. Even though he was exhausted, he doubted he'd get much sleep tonight, but had to try. He loved Taylor's tea idea.

However, when he turned the corner, he stopped cold in his tracks.

The contorted expression on her face as she studied her phone told him even the tea wouldn't help.

"What is it, Taylor?"

"This." She swiveled her phone around and shoved it closer to him.

He read the text message, his pulse ratcheting up for the umpteenth time today. "How did they get your phone number?"

She shrugged. "Good question, but you'd be surprised at how hackers can easily gain access in today's world. There are so many scams out there, preying on innocent victims."

"Block this number." He slid the phone back in her direction.

"Already did. Also forwarded it to Bryan."

Wyatt picked up her box of chamomile-lavender tea. "Will this help?"

She massaged her neck. "Doubtful, but I'm willing to try. I need to put this day behind me."

"Me, too." He observed Shadow snoozing on a stack of towels in the corner. "I see he likes to stay close."

"He does, so I found the towels in the hall closet. Hope that was okay."

"Of course. My casa is your casa."

"Levi asleep?"

"Yep. Didn't even get to the second line of his favorite story."

"Which is?"

"David and Goliath." The irony wasn't lost on Wyatt that his son's favorite story was from the Bible and had also been Wyatt's. "And yes, I know what you're thinking. Odd that I read to him from the Bible when I struggle to read it myself."

She lifted her hands in a surrender position. "Not saying anything."

"But you're probably thinking it." He shuffled into her personal space and tapped her temple. "I remember how your brain works."

She drew in a sharp breath at his sudden action, her gaze locking with his.

Even though he figured she was as tired as he was, she still looked stunning—just like the first day they'd met. It wasn't only her smile that had drawn his attention back then—and now—but her dazzling blue eyes. Blue as the ocean and he couldn't help getting lost in their lure.

The kettle shrieked, intruding on their moment.

Saved by the whistle. Good thing. In his tired state, Wyatt didn't trust his emotions. He fell hard for her once before and didn't plan on that happening again.

Taylor cleared her throat and turned the burner off. "Grab a couple of mugs and we'll get this tea brewing. It's late, but we're obviously both still keyed up after a stressful day. Let's have a seat. I'd like to hear what you've been up to for the past two years."

He loved how she made herself at home, even if it stung because he realized they'd both move on with their lives after

Ridge's arrest and imprisonment. She proved the last time that she wasn't interested in a relationship with Wyatt.

Why was he suddenly wanting that relationship back again?

Ugh! Get it together. You're tired. That's what this is. Exhaustion.

But was it?

He buried the questions racing through his head and whipped open the cupboard door, bringing out two plaid mugs as he examined his backyard. All appeared to be quiet, but the earlier threat on their lives tumbled into his mind. Was someone out there watching? Studying their every move? He prayed that wasn't the case, but the warning on Taylor's phone proved Ridge wasn't about to quit searching for them. He set the mugs on the counter. *Stop. No one followed you home.* Wyatt was a private person and liked his solitude, so only a few people knew where he lived.

After fixing their tea, they sat at Wyatt's dining room table.

Taylor set her phone down beside her and dunked her tea bag multiple times in her mug. "Now that we're not running for our lives, tell me how you've been."

Wyatt stared into his mug, gathering his thoughts. "Levi and I have been doing well. Lots happening in my family. Some good, some not so good."

"Like what?"

"Well, we recently discovered that we have another sister we didn't know about."

Taylor stilled, her cup midway to her mouth. "What?"

"Yep. I guess Violet had a twin that Mom and Dad were told had died at birth, but Baylee was stolen and sold to an unsuspecting family. Illegal adoption."

"Wow. I keep hearing of that happening more often than we'd like to believe. I'm sure that was a shock for Violet."

"Yes. For all of us. Speaking of my parents, I have to call them and explain what's going on. Mom is a prayer warrior and even though I'm not, I would like her on her knees." Wyatt sipped his tea, desperate for it to calm his nerves. "Enough about me. Why did you move back from Nova Scotia? Didn't you like it there?"

Her eyes darkened seconds before her gaze shifted to her tea sitting on the table in front of her, but he didn't miss the switch of emotions.

"What is it, Taylor? Did something happen?" He set his mug down and placed his hand on top of hers. "You can tell me. I'm a good listener."

She withdrew her hand and chewed on her bottom lip. Stalling or gathering thoughts?

He waited, letting the silence settle in the room.

Taylor wheezed in a breath. "I almost lost Shadow."

Not the answer he'd been expecting. He had wondered if a man broke her heart like she had his. "I'm so sorry. What happened?"

"We had three abductions of young children, and each time they went missing, Shadow found and saved them. The parents were all so grateful and the media caught wind of it. They did a feature on us on the six o'clock news."

Wyatt eyed the dog in the corner.

The K-9's ears twitched, and he opened one eye because he knew they were talking about him.

"He's good at what he does." Wyatt shifted his gaze back to Taylor. "I imagine he became popular."

"Too popular for my liking. That's when this ring targeted him. They weren't done kidnapping and wanted him out of the picture."

"What happened?"

"We fell for a fake child abduction and they almost killed Shadow." Taylor's reply hissed out a boatload of emotions.

Shadow woofed, hopped onto all fours and trotted to her side, snuggling close. She bent down and pressed her face into his. "Sorry, boy. Didn't mean to scare you."

Wyatt's heart melted at the duo's obvious love for one another. "You have a strong bond, don't you?"

"Yes, and I went into an awful place at the thought that I almost lost him." She kissed Shadow's head. "Someone called into 911 stating a missing child was trapped in a container at a shipping yard, and they needed the infamous Shadow to find him. We began a search when a sniper tried to take him out." Taylor rubbed the dog's ears. "But they underestimated all of Shadow's abilities and he sensed the danger."

"What happened?"

"He shifted just as the bullet pinged off the concrete and we took cover."

Wyatt whistled. "Did they catch the sniper?"

"They did. Their plan backfired. Instead of Shadow finding a missing boy, he led us right to the sniper." She sipped her tea. "Joke was on them."

"So why would that make you move?"

Taylor ran her fingers around the ring of her mug. "I just wanted to come home. A new position came available with the constabulary. K-9 handler team lead. I jumped at the chance to work with Bryan."

"Plus, I'm sure you're glad to be close to your mom again. How's your relationship with her?"

She pursed her lips. "I'd rather not talk about Mom, but let's just say she hasn't been totally truthful throughout my life."

That didn't sound good, but he was tired and didn't want to probe her any further. "Well, I'm glad you're back. Thanks to you and Shadow for saving my son."

Lightning flashed through the dining room window, followed by a crack of thunder.

"Great, the storm has returned. Let's hope—"

The lights snapped out.

Levi let out a bloodcurdling scream.

Shadow barked and tore out of the dining room.

Wyatt bolted out of his chair, groping in the darkness to get to his son.

The ranch was secure, so Wyatt guessed Levi's scream came from nightmares and storms.

Even so, Wyatt wouldn't leave his son's side tonight.

Taylor's breath hitched as another flash of lightning illuminated the room. She snatched her phone off the table and turned on the flashlight, shining the spotlight to help guide their way up the stairs. She followed Wyatt into Levi's room.

He raced to his crying son's side and brought him into his arms. "It's okay, bud. I'm here."

"Bad...man." Levi's two words came out between sobs.

Taylor shone the light around, searching for intruders, but only shadows filled the room. She opened the closet door and parted the hanging clothes to ensure no one was hiding behind them. Nothing. The room was empty.

Wyatt rubbed Levi's back. "It's just a dream, son. The bad man isn't here. You're okay. I've got you."

The compassion between father and son struck a chord in Taylor, and she struggled to fight the growing feelings. *Leave before it's too late.*

But how could she when she had been tasked to remain by their side? She'd do what she did best.

Taylor straightened and rolled her shoulders, determination setting in. She'd treat the pair as she did any other she'd been assigned to protect.

A client—so to speak.

Compartmentalize. She had to. It was the only way she'd get through this. Her heart wouldn't survive crushing his all over again. Once was enough. She barely escaped the pit of despair she'd fallen into two years ago.

She placed her hand on her abdomen, reminding her of the reason she'd never date. She couldn't stomach the idea of not being able to bear children. Wyatt came from a large family, and he'd shared he wanted more kids one day.

Tears prickled at the back of her eyes.

Shadow rubbed against her legs. He sensed some type of battle going on inside his handler, and he wanted to make it better.

Taylor pinched the bridge of her nose, forcing the tears to remain at bay, and inched closer to the bed. "Levi, do you know that I'm not only a dog handler, but a policewoman, too?"

His mouth hung open. "You are? Where's your cowgirl hat?"

She chuckled. "I don't have one of those, but I checked your room and the bad man isn't here. You're safe now. Shadow and I will make sure of it."

He yawned. "Thanks."

Wyatt mouthed *thank you* to Taylor before tucking his son back in under the covers. "Time to sleep, bud."

The boy reached his tiny hand out from under his superhero bedspread. "Papa, stay."

Taylor smiled as she contemplated how this six-foot man would fit into Levi's twin-size bed.

As if sensing her thoughts, Wyatt glanced over his shoulder, winked at her and crawled in beside his son, nestling close.

Her breath hitched at the sight. There was nothing more touching than a father holding his child in love and protection. *Just like You hold Your children, right, Lord?* Her head knew that to be true, but her heart was slow to believe in God's unconditional love at times. Could He love her even when she doubted and didn't always trust Him in the storms of life?

Another flicker of lightning flashed under Levi's bedroom blinds.

Was that God's response to her thoughts? *Okay, I hear You.*

"Night," she whispered as she backed out of the room, silently commanding Shadow to come. Time to let father and son sleep.

Taylor meandered her way to the guest bedroom and sank down onto the bed. Her weary body required sleep, but could she silence her brain from thoughts of a killer targeting them and the two males down the hall?

She had to in order to survive.

Wyatt wrestled to wake from dreams of kidnappers and the ringing going on in his head. A dog barked somewhere close. Shadow? What was that annoying bell?

He jerked upright and rolled off the bed, thudding to the floor. Ugh! He forgot that he slept with his son, but his aching back reminded him. Being stuck in one position hadn't helped.

Shadow barked again.

Banging sounded from the ranch's lower level.

Someone was at the door. *Get it together, Wyatt.* He placed his hands on his son's bed and pushed himself upright before stumbling into the hallway.

Shadow and a sleepy Taylor puttered out of the guest room.

Taylor had dressed in a pair of Iris's jeans and a pink plaid shirt—Lisa's shirt.

He choked in an audible breath.

Taylor stopped mid-step. "What?"

Wyatt waggled his finger at her. "Where did you get that shirt?" He failed to suppress the annoyance in his question.

"The closet. Isn't it one of Iris's?"

He swallowed the thickening in his throat. "No. It's Lisa's."

Her jaw dropped. "So sorry. I'll go change right away. I just assumed it was your sister's since it was in the guest room."

Lisa had been gone for four years now, but that was her favorite shirt, and he hadn't been able to give it away with the rest of her clothing. The color suited Taylor. Could he let her wear it? The battle over whether he should raged in his mind. *Let go.*

He puffed out a breath and raised his hands. "No, it's okay. You can wear it."

"Are you sure?"

He nodded.

The doorbell rang.

"I gotta get that." Wyatt checked his watch. "Wait, how could it be ten thirty? I never sleep this late."

"Me neither. We obviously needed it."

Shadow woofed and bolted around them, running down the stairs.

"Were you expecting anyone?" Taylor rubbed her eyes.

"Hux was going to retrieve our packs, but I'm not sure he'd be able to do that this quickly." Wyatt followed Shadow.

"Wait up," Taylor said. "We have to be cautious."

Wyatt reached Shadow and peeked through the front door's side glass panel. "Yep, it's Hux." He unlocked the door and the extra dead bolt, then pushed it open. "You're early."

Park Warden Hux Price entered the foyer carrying their backpacks. "Sorry, did I wake you? I figured you'd want these right away." He held them out.

Wyatt took the packs and set them on a nearby mat. "Thank you. How early did you hike up to the gorge?"

"You know how much I love a good sunrise, so I left before dawn. Took me a few minutes to find them, though. You were smart in hiding them. I still can't believe they used the red bridge to construct that pulley system."

"I know. Seems that they are re—"

Taylor cleared her throat.

Shadow let out a low-pitched growl in response to his handler's tone.

He caught her clear warning. *Don't talk about the case. We can't trust anyone.*

But Hux wasn't just anyone. He was Wyatt's best friend.

Wyatt rubbed his temples. "Hux, would you like to come in for a coffee?"

"Can't. Have to get back to work."

"Thanks for these." Taylor scooped up her bag. "Wyatt, I'll put on some coffee." She disappeared into the kitchen.

Shadow trotted after her.

"That's my cue." Hux placed his hand on the doorknob. "One more thing. Cam hiked up there with me and said something strange earlier."

The hairs prickled at the back of Wyatt's neck. He didn't like the sound of that. "What?"

"That he wasn't surprised someone kidnapped Levi, and that you had it coming."

Wyatt's mouth grew parched. "Why would he say that?"

"No idea." He opened the door. "Just wanted to warn you. Don't trust that man."

"Thanks for the heads-up. Talk later and thanks again."

Hux dashed down the steps. "No prob. Chow, bro."

Wyatt scanned the front yard before closing and locking the door. Even though his ranch was well hidden, he couldn't shake the feeling that someone was watching them.

And Cam Field knew exactly where Wyatt lived.

EIGHT

Wyatt set a stack of two chocolate chip pancakes in front of his sleepy-eyed son. "As promised, Mr. Hoyt."

Levi giggled. "I'm not a mister, Papa."

Wyatt stared at Taylor.

Her smile curling behind the hand over her mouth told him she was struggling to subdue a laugh.

Wyatt picked up his knife and fork. "Well, you are five now."

"Five and a half. And tallest in my class, Papa." Levi snatched the maple syrup and poured a steady stream of the goodness over his stack.

"Whoa, son. That's plenty." Wyatt took the bottle and passed it to Taylor. "We sure are lazybones today, aren't we?"

"I rarely sleep past eight, let alone ten thirty. I'm surprised Sergeant Mitchell hasn't called me yet since I haven't checked in." Taylor buttered her pancakes and poured syrup on top. "Okay, who's saying grace?"

Levi's hand shot up. "Me! G'pa taught me."

Guilt locked Wyatt's muscles. After Lisa's death, Wyatt had stopped taking Levi to church. Lisa had been the faith warrior in their home, and without her, Wyatt was left clinging to his frayed thread of faith. Truth be told, that thread had snapped after the numbness of her funeral subsided.

Wyatt pushed the memory away and bowed his head. "Go ahead, Levi."

"God, bless this food to our tummies. Help the pancakes make us stronger. And catch that bad man. Amen." Levi stabbed his pancakes with his fork and stuffed a huge bite into his mouth.

"Amen," Wyatt and Taylor said together.

"Son, slow down." Wyatt cut into his pancake. "We don't have to rush off anywhere. No kindergarten for today, okay?"

"Can… I…watch…spidy…man…cartoon?" he asked, mumbling between bites.

"Of course. Maybe we can have popcorn and watch it together."

Levi's eyes lit up. "Shadow, too?"

Wyatt's gaze shifted to Taylor. "Well? What do you think?"

"Sure, but after we have our chat and I update my boss."

He nodded.

"Papa, where's my milk?" Levi asked.

"Right. I forgot." Wyatt got up and grabbed the milk from the fridge, pouring Levi a glass. His son always requested milk whenever they had pancakes. It was his fave.

Wyatt set a glass in front of Levi. "There you go."

Ten minutes later, Wyatt set his fork down and nudged his plate away, clasping his fingers together. "Levi, Taylor and I need to ask you some questions about yesterday. Is that okay?"

The five-year-old's lips quivered.

Taylor reached across the table and placed her hand on top of Levi's. "It's okay if you can't, but it will help me and Daddy to catch the bad man. I'll put him in prison, but I can't do that without your help. Would you like to be my police partner?"

Wyatt smiled at Taylor's gentleness and creativity. She was good with children. If only—

He gritted his teeth. *Nope, not going there.*

Levi's mouth hung open. "Will I get a badge? Gun?"

Taylor chuckled. "I could probably make you a badge, but I'm pretty sure your father wouldn't approve of a gun. What do you think? Can you tell us what happened?"

He nodded.

Taylor removed her hand and popped to her feet. "Just a second." She plucked a coiled notebook out of her bag before sitting back down. "Ready." She dipped her chin toward Wyatt, silently asking him to begin.

They had to start off gently.

"Son, why did Aunt Denise take you to that park?" Wyatt had to find out the answer to the question plaguing him.

"I wanted to play hide-and-seek, Papa. It's my favorite park. I'm sorry." Tears moistened his eyes. "Did Aunty D die because of me?"

"Oh, Levi. Of course not. It's not your fault." Wyatt shoved his chair out and brought his son into his arms. "Don't ever think that. Okay?"

Levi sniffed. "'Kay."

"Can you tell us what happened when you played hide-and-seek?" Taylor's question brought them back to the room.

Wyatt released Levi.

"It was my turn to hide, but the bad men were yelling down the trail. Aunty D told me to hide in the trees. I saw her taking pictures."

"Did you hear what the men said?" Taylor asked.

"The bad man yelled and asked for money. Other man said no." Levi gulped in an audible breath.

"Have a drink, son. Take your time."

Levi obeyed and finished his glass of milk before continuing. "The bad man shot the other guy. Aunty D jumped into the bushes and hid with me. A few seconds later, the man stopped by us yelling that he'd find whoever was hiding. Aunty D covered my mouth so I wouldn't say anything. The man said a bad word and then ran off. His phone fell out of his pocket in front of us where we were hiding."

"Did he see you?" Wyatt's muscles locked at the idea.

"I don't know."

"Did you see his face, son?" Wyatt held his breath.

"I did, but he had sunglasses on. We waited until he was gone and then came out of our hiding spot. Aunty D picked up the phone, and we walked to the other guy. He was dead."

The message to "run" flashed in Wyatt's mind. "Did he know you were there, and that's why he carved the message to run?"

Levi shrugged. "Maybe."

Taylor let out a sharp cry, revealing she had the same thought as Wyatt.

The phone must be what Ridge was after. "Son, where is the phone?"

"Aunty D gave me both phones and told me to take them to you, but I didn't want the bad man's, so I hid it in a tree. I should have kept it. I'm sorry, Papa." His lips quivered again.

"It's okay, son. What happened next?" Wyatt had to finish the conversation before his son's emotions spiraled out of control.

"We heard the bad man again, so she pushed me into the bushes." He lifted his sleeve. "That's when I cut my arm, but I stopped the bleeding like you taught me."

"Good boy. Proud of you. What happened next?"

"Aunty D told me to stay and not to come out until you came, Papa."

"But you didn't. Why?" Wyatt kept his tone low and gentle. He didn't want his son to think he was angry for not obeying his aunt.

"Aunty D didn't hide, Papa. She tried to fight the bad man and then ran."

Denise had sacrificed her life by drawing attention away from her nephew. *Thank you, Denise.*

Why, God? Why would You allow her to die for such a courageous act?

Wyatt fiddled with his utensils, focusing hard not to cry.

"Levi, can you tell us what came after that?" Taylor rested her hand on Wyatt's, stilling his jitters. She had read the battle going on inside him and silently offered her sympathy.

"Aunty D ran and the man followed. I waited for her to come back, but only the bad man did with other bad men."

Wyatt's curiosity returned to his son. "Other men?"

"Hunters, Papa. They were looking for the phone."

Levi's drawing entered Wyatt's mind. "Did you hear what else they said? Why did you draw that picture?"

"To show you what they said about a red bridge and a plane."

"And the bow and arrow? Why did you draw it funny? Did you see it?"

Levi nodded. "It looked like my superhero's not like yours in the barn. The bad man said he had lots more in a box at the red bridge."

Wyatt resisted the urge to bang his fist on the table, but his son's account confirmed what they'd suspected. He witnessed both a murder and a weapon smuggling deal gone wrong. "Levi, did Aunty D take a picture of the bow and arrow?"

"Yes. Did you find her phone? I left it for you, Papa."

"We did. Taylor, it's in your backpack. Can you get it?"

She hopped up to where her pack sat on the counter, fished out the device, and passed it to Wyatt.

Wyatt placed it in front of his son. "We found all of your clues, too. I'm so proud of you. You did what your grandfather taught you."

"G'pa told me to leave breadcrumbs when I was lost."

"You are so smart, Levi," Taylor said. "You're a top-notch police officer."

His eyes grew the size of saucers. "I am?"

Taylor smiled. "You are. This will help us find the bad man."

Wyatt pointed to the phone. "Aunty D let you play on her phone. Do you know her code?"

Levi picked it up and tapped on it. "Mama's name and birdday. *L-I-S-A*-3-1-1." He emphasized each letter and number as he entered the code.

The phone came to life, and an image appeared on the screen.

A picture of a man dressed in camouflage, bandana over his mouth and wearing sunglasses. Ridge.

Terror seized Wyatt's muscles. Not only had Levi taken Ridge's phone, but now they had his picture.

No wonder Ridge targeted them.

Taylor acknowledged the fear contorting Wyatt's face—she felt it, too, pummeling through her with the same intensity.

Denise had obviously captured pictures that could be used against Ridge, but did Ridge know that fact? He also assumed they had his device.

But they didn't. Not yet. They had to find it before he did.

Wyatt had taken Levi into their family room and put on a movie for him. Taylor had tasked Shadow to protect Levi, so the German shepherd jumped up beside the boy and snuggled close. Taylor and Wyatt would join him later, but right now they sat at the kitchen table with another coffee, ready to search Denise's phone.

Wyatt set the device between them. "Okay, let's see what pictures Denise took." He clicked on the photo icon and swiped through the images. Two of the masked hunter, and another of the deceased male. More of the weapons.

"Only the hunter and the buyer were at this deal gone wrong." Taylor pointed to the video. "Did she catch the exchange? Click that."

Wyatt hit the arrow button.

A video displayed with the hunter's back to the camera and the buyer in the distance. Denise had zoomed in for a better view, but the sound wasn't the best quality. Only snippets of words every now and then were audible. Deal. Exchange. Weapons. However, one aspect of the exchange came through loud and clear via the buyer's body language. His arms flailed in the air.

"That's not the price we agreed on." The angered statement came out louder this time.

Denise must have turned up the volume. Taylor leaned in, paying close attention.

"You. Pay or the deal is off." The seller's voice softened but his harshness remained.

"You renege, then I go to the cops. I know your dirty secrets, Ridge."

"Suit yourself." Ridge mumbled a few more words before yanking out his gun and shooting the buyer.

A gasp sailed through the video.

"Who's there?" Ridge turned slightly at the sound, but not enough to get a clear picture of his face, but she caught a glimpse of the sunglasses Levi had mentioned.

The video ended without warning.

"Denise's reaction gave her away," Taylor said.

"No wonder she told Levi to stay hidden." Wyatt's twisted expression revealed his elevated state.

"Did you recognize Ridge's voice? Play it again."

Wyatt hit the button and turned up the volume, listening close. After the video ended, he shook his head. "The voice is too hoarse and strained. I can make out a few of the words, but it sounds like he's trying to disguise his voice. Why would he do that? He didn't realize Denise was filming this until later."

Lightning flashed through the dining room window, followed by a crack of thunder.

Great. Another storm. Just what they needed.

"Good question. Perhaps the buyer doesn't know his true identity, and he's trying to keep it that way."

"His stance seems familiar, but I can't place why." Wyatt jerked to his feet, clenching his hands while he paced. "It's on the tip of my tongue. Close but far. Ugh!"

"Don't force the memory. It will come naturally."

He spun around and faced her head-on. "What do we do next? I can't just sit here and wait for this Ridge person to attack us. He probably thinks Levi can identify him."

"We need that other phone that Levi hid. There may be something on it to help us figure out who Ridge is and what he's planning next."

Wyatt plunked into his chair and motioned toward the window. "But bad weather has returned. Hux got to the gorge just in time today."

"Yes, thankfully. Meteorologists are suggesting this storm will have even more hail than yesterday's. Not a good combination."

Wyatt hissed out a breath. "Especially in the mountains."

"Then we wait. Bryan told me to lie low today anyway."

Wyatt slapped his palm onto the table. "I feel so helpless. I should be able to protect my own son."

"Wyatt, don't go there." Taylor had to keep his mind occupied while they waited out the storm. "Can you tell me anything more about the smuggling ring you stopped four years ago? Do you think it's the same person?"

"Possibly. I never saw the two men's faces. They were too far away when they were on the bridge. I reported what I had found, and the police took it from there. I wasn't involved after that. Could you find something in your records?"

"Yes, I was going to do that. Thanks for the reminder." She hopped to her feet and snatched her laptop off the counter, carrying it back to the table.

Her cell phone rang, and she read the screen. "That's Bryan. I have to take this."

"I'll go check on Levi and then make us more coffee." He shuffled out of the room.

Taylor hit Answer. "Morning, Bryan."

"Well, it's almost lunchtime. Why haven't you called?"

She cringed. "I'm sorry. I meant to, but we all slept in late. Then Wyatt made pancakes. Didn't have time." She was rambling. *Get it together.*

"Please tell me nothing else happened after that threatening text."

"No. Did digital forensics get anything from it?"

"Unknown number. We're guessing it came from a burner phone. Have you interrogated Levi yet?"

"Yes." She updated him on the conversation, the hidden phone, and what they found in Denise's photo library.

"We have to get our hands on that other phone. Did Levi say where it was?"

"In a tree close to where he hid."

"The weather is supposed to clear tomorrow, so maybe he could show you."

Taylor tapped her thumb on the table. "I'm not sure that's wise, sir, or that Wyatt would even consider the option. He wouldn't want to put his son at risk again."

"Since you mentioned he's good at drawing, perhaps he could draw a map. Wyatt knows that park well."

"True. Today, I want to look through our records for that investigation on a smuggling ring from four years ago. It may give us more details."

"Sounds good."

Wyatt returned and poured water into the coffee carafe.

"Gotta run, sir. Keep me posted on any findings."

"Will do. You as well. Please be careful. Stay there. I have cruisers patrolling."

"Copy. Bye for now." She ended the call. "Levi okay?"

"Found him and Shadow fast asleep." He chuckled as he added coffee beans to his machine. "I restarted the movie for him and promised popcorn. What did your sergeant say?"

She gave him the update while she signed in to her station's records. She searched through the files, adding in the dates from four years ago.

No records found displayed.

She bristled. "What? Impossible."

Wyatt stepped forward. "What is it?"

"Can you confirm I used the right dates?" She pointed to her screen.

"Try two days before. I know because it was right before Lisa's accident."

Taylor adjusted her query and hit Enter.

This time, the screen flashed a different message.

Records deleted.

The date and time of the deletion displayed beside the message.

This morning.

Two minutes ago.

Taylor's chest tightened.

Not only had the files been deleted today, but it had to have been someone within the police department. And moments after she'd spoken to her sergeant.

No! She would not believe it was him.

But she also couldn't deny the suspicious timing.

NINE

"I know what you're thinking." Wyatt grabbed their mugs and walked to the coffee machine, pouring them each a fresh cup. He set hers in front of her and sat. "Do you really think your sergeant would delete police records?"

"No, but I also can't deny the timing. I just finished telling him I was going to look the records up and they're gone within minutes after our call."

"Does it give any type of ID who deleted them, and is it even possible to do that with official records?" Wyatt sipped his hazelnut coffee.

"Not that I can see." She hit a number on her cell phone and put the call on speaker. "There has to be an explanation for this. Maybe he looked them up and accidentally deleted them. Let's find out."

Wyatt doubted that was the case, but kept the thought to himself. He could tell Sergeant Mitchell meant the world to Taylor, and he wasn't about to add suspicion on top of her already confused state of mind.

"Taylor. You forget something?" The amusement in Mitchell's voice filtered through the phone.

"Sir, I'm here with Wyatt. I have a question. Did you delete the records from four years ago related to the smuggling ring?"

Silence.

"Sir?"

"How could you ask such a question, Taylor? After everything we've been through together." His hurt tone came through loud and clear.

"The timing is suspicious, sir. Someone deleted them two

minutes after our conversation when I told you I was looking them up."

Silence again.

Taylor stopped mid-motion of stirring creamer into her coffee. "You still there?"

"Yes. I was looking it up myself. You're right. The files are gone. It. Was. Not. Me." He paused. "I would never delete police records."

"I believe you, and I'm sorry." Taylor hung her head. "I didn't think it was you, but had to ask."

"I get it. The timing is definitely questionable, but rest assured, I will get Digital Forensics on it."

"Sergeant Mitchell, any ideas on who would delete them?" Wyatt sipped his coffee.

"My door wasn't closed, so anyone here at the station may have heard our conversation. I had put you on speaker as I was working on paperwork at the same time."

Taylor gnawed on her fingernail before jerking her hand away. "Wyatt, do you remember what officer you spoke to when you reported everything back then?"

Wyatt rubbed his temples as if that would spark his memory from four years ago at a time in his life he'd rather forget. "That was just days before Lisa's accident, so my mind is fuzzy, but I'm pretty sure it was an older gentleman who said he was retiring."

"That would have been Constable Fred Atkins," Mitchell said. "He's the only one in our station that's retired in the last few years."

"We have to speak with him. Does he still live in the area, sir?" Taylor asked.

"No, he moved to Regina to live with his ailing sister. He's not that techy, but you could probably still connect with him via video conference. I'll send you his email."

"Good. That's something we can do from here. Thanks, sir. I'm sorry for doubting you."

"It's okay. I understand why you would. Be sure to share what you find out from old Freddy."

"Will do."

Voices sounded in the background. "Wait, Taylor. The report on the constable's interrogation of that suspect from yesterday came in seconds ago. Reading it now."

Hope surged through Wyatt's veins and he gripped his mug tighter, his knee bouncing in anticipation.

"Here's what this guy told us. Apparently, there's a huge deal going down at the gorge. Major shipment. One other thing. Wyatt, this guy said your son was targeted purposely. Ridge has been watching both of you."

Wyatt's knee stopped bouncing as dread cemented every muscle in his body. "Where? When? But how did he know Levi was going to be at the park?"

"That he didn't know, but he assumed that when Ridge realized Denise and Levi were there, it played right into his plan."

Taylor leaned forward. "His plan?"

"That's all the suspect knew. Wyatt, Ridge has to be someone who knows you. Have you made enemies with anyone recently? Someone who would want to target Levi to get back at you?"

Wyatt wracked his brain to make sense of it all. "No. Other than whoever I had stopped four years ago at the red bridge. I'm guessing it's this person they call Ridge. Did the suspect know his identity?"

"No. Apparently, they wear masks when they're together. The suspect said that only Ridge's right-hand man knows who he really is."

"When is the deal going down?" Taylor asked.

"He didn't know the exact day and time. Wyatt, we need that other phone. I'm going to work at getting a warrant, so we'll be ready. I realize it's a huge ask, but can Levi lead you to where he hid it? It's the fastest way."

"But not the safest. I get it. We need the phone, but this is my son's life we're talking about." Wyatt's heart rate increased at the idea of putting him back in the crosshairs of a killer.

"I can show you, Papa." Levi entered the kitchen with Shadow at his heels. "I know a shortcut. Please. Can I help catch the bad man? Remember, I'm Miss Taylor's partner." His eyes grew wide, pleading with his father.

Those eyes—Lisa's eyes.

Wyatt's breath hitched. His son knew which buttons to push.

"We can bring in more constables to keep you all safe," Mitchell said.

"And the storm is supposed to break overnight," Taylor added. "Shadow will keep us safe, too."

"Papa, I want popcorn. Shadow, come." Levi whirled around and hustled out of the room, Shadow trotting behind him.

Wyatt chuckled at his son's command. "I guess I'm outnumbered." He lifted his index finger. "One condition. Any—and I mean any—signs of danger and we get out of the forest."

"Understood. Taylor, contact Freddy and see what information you can get from him. Maybe something new will pop. In the meantime, I'll task two constables I trust to escort you into the park tomorrow morning." More voices sailed through the speaker. "Listen, I gotta go. Stay safe."

"You, too." Taylor ended the call. "Wyatt, you okay?"

"I'm not sure what to make of this new intel."

"My sergeant will help us get to the bottom of it. I knew it couldn't be him who deleted those records. He's a by-the-book officer."

"So you believe him?"

She scrunched up her nose. "You don't? How can you say that when you don't know him like I do?"

Wyatt hissed out a breath. "You're right. I'm just suspicious of everyone right now with Levi's life on the line."

"I get it. Sorry for being sensitive and protective of the man. He's done a lot for me." She stood and took her coffee over to the window, peering out. "It's raining quite hard. Looks like we're stuck here for now."

"Is it such a bad thing to be stuck with me?" Did he really ask that question out loud? *Way to go, Wyatt. You just placed that proverbial elephant in the room.*

She pivoted, her eyes wide. "Of course not. I didn't mean to imply that. Only—"

He raised his right hand in a stop position. "I'm kidding. I don't know why I said that. I've missed our conversations. We had amazing talks when we were dating." *And now you're rambling. You can't leave it alone, can you?* He clamped his mouth shut. Wyatt had too much on his mind to even think straight right now.

"It's okay, Wyatt. I agree. We did and we still can now that I'm back. You were a good friend to me." She returned to her seat at the table.

Friend? Was that all she had ever considered him? A good friend? He stifled the irritation growing inside, counting to five. He had to put her out of his head and change the conversation.

Her laptop dinged.

She wiggled her mouse. "Bryan sent Fred's email. I'll contact him now. Hopefully, he'll reply soon."

Good. Saved by the bell. Again.

Taylor tapped on her keyboard as she chewed on her lip. Something he had noted and loved. The habit was cute on her.

Stop it. Friends, remember? He had to get away from her, if only for a few minutes. Reboot his mind, so to speak.

"I'm going to make popcorn for Levi while you do that." Wyatt placed his hands on the table and pushed himself up. He didn't trust his wobbly legs even after a good night's rest. That plunge into the water and bullet nick had taken more out of him than he cared to admit. Maybe it was a good thing it was storming outside. It forced him to stay indoors, but he had to contact his supervisor or he'd never hear the end of it.

After making popcorn for Levi and calling his folks to update them on the situation, Wyatt entered his office. His mother had promised to get on her knees and lift them in prayer. The thought soothed Wyatt, even though his doubts about God plagued him.

He closed the door and picked up his landline receiver, punching in Supervisor Bain's number.

"Bain here." His gruff voice revealed irritation.

Wyatt grimaced. Not a great start. "Sir, it's Wyatt checking in."

"'Bout time you called. I realize I let you take today, but you were supposed to update me. I needed to ensure you're safe."

Even though the man could be rough, he cared about his employees, especially Field, but Bain had a funny way of showing it. "Sorry, sir. Yesterday weighed heavily on us and we had a late start to the day. Anything new on your end? More reports of those smugglers in our parks?"

Newfoundland had several provincial parks and a few national ones. Conservation officers patrolled all to ensure wildlife and visitor safety.

"Nothing yet, but Cam is on the job. He's the best, so he'll find those responsible."

Wyatt flinched at the man's obvious favoritism and bit back a retort. He couldn't afford to get back on the man's bad side. Wyatt had struggled to maintain a healthy relationship with Supervisor Bain after not being able to catch the ring four years ago. He had blamed Wyatt and never let him forget.

Even though Wyatt had done everything by the book, his boss had failed to see it that way.

"I'm still waiting for your report from yesterday's events. You can log in from your ranch and file it." Voices muttered in the background. "Wait, Cam is here and wants to tell you something."

"Wyatt, just came in from patrolling your area of Teragoose Park. I found a note pinned to a tree with an arrow. It's a message for you."

Wyatt stiffened. "What does it say?"

"'You can't hide forever, Wyatt Hoyt. You're a dead man, along with your son and girlfriend.'"

Wyatt's stomach coiled like a rattlesnake, ready to strike. He knew it was only a matter of time until Ridge found him. A thought entered his mind, and he rolled his shoulders back, courage setting in.

He would find Ridge first and stop him this time.

Even if he died protecting his son, saving Levi was Wyatt's top priority.

Taylor's senses prickled as she entered Teragoose National Park's forest the next morning, especially after Wyatt updated her on Ridge's latest threat. She surveyed the area, checking for any suspicious activity, but so far, the path was empty of animals and humans. Taylor had dropped by the police station to get new gear to replace what she had on her when they took a plunge into the river. Sergeant Mitchell had provided them with new cell phones and had also given her permission to keep her gun at the ranch, issuing her a locked box to put it in. He didn't want her unarmed. He still hadn't discovered who had deleted the files, but was interrogating his constables and civilian employees to get to the bottom of it. Bryan warned Taylor not to trust anyone until he could apprehend those responsible for the breach. She wasn't taking any chances today and commanded Shadow to stick close to Levi.

She turned to the two constables Bryan had tasked to protect the group. The sergeant had also put Taylor in charge. "Be alert. These hunters are ruthless. We have to keep our heads on a swivel."

Constable Samantha Day tilted her head and placed her hands on her hips. "We know how to do our jobs, Grant."

Taylor quelled her thoughts of frustration toward Day. They had butted heads years ago when they'd worked together and it seemed like the thirty-year-old still held grudges over their leader's *favoritism*—as she called it—toward Taylor. Taylor had tried to explain how their sergeant had stepped into the role of a father for Taylor since her own had left when she was a child. While at the station, Taylor and Bryan had kept their special bond professional, but Day failed to see it that way.

Taylor raised her hands in a surrender position. Best contain the situation right here, right now. "I know that, Day, but we saw firsthand what these hunters are capable of and—" she gestured toward Levi "—this boy's life is in our hands."

"We get it, Grant, and we'll stay close." Constable Gavin Elliott repositioned himself beside the boy, flanking him on the opposite side of Shadow.

"And we're here to help, too." Conservation Officer Cam Field trotted up the path with Warden Price and another man. "I brought reinforcements."

Taylor held out her hand to the dark, wavy-haired man with the mustache and goatee. "Constable Taylor Grant. You are?"

He shook her hand with gusto. "Park guide, Asher Calloway. Call me Ash." He shifted to face Wyatt head-on. "We'll do everything we can to keep your son safe."

Taylor eyed the silent Wyatt and guessed from his taut body language that he was battling his decision to bring Levi. It was a risk, and they all realized it, but after he came out of his office yesterday, he had a new determination on his face. He promised he would find Ridge before he found them. After they both finished their reports, they enjoyed the rest of the day watching movies with Levi. Just like a family.

If only.

Wyatt blinked rapidly before nodding. "I appreciate you all being here." He adjusted his cowboy hat and duty belt before bending in front of his son. "Levi, where did you hide the phone?"

"Close to our favorite cave. I can show you. Papa, God is with us. This way!" Levi hurried down the path to the right.

Shadow barked and bounded behind him.

"Wait up, son." Wyatt jogged after the energetic five-year-old.

"Let's split into groups." Taylor pointed to the trail on the left. "Day, you go with Cam and Asher that way. Elliott and Hux, you stay with the rest of us."

"Why would you split us up when the boy knows where he hid it?" Day's eyes betrayed her obvious defiance at Taylor's suggestion.

"Because even though this boy is extremely smart, we must protect him from all angles. Trust me, those hunters are out there somewhere and we have to surround Levi from all vantage points." When would this woman ever trust in Taylor's instincts and abilities? She only wanted to cover Levi and Wyatt in a blanket of protection.

Even though she realized it was more than that.

Much more.

Taylor's feelings for both had reemerged in the short time she'd been with the duo. She couldn't deny that fact, but she must contain those feelings or history would repeat itself like a bad groundhog day.

She couldn't do that to Wyatt again.

Or herself.

Taylor cleared her throat. "Please listen to me. I know what I'm doing." And she was in charge, but she'd keep that extra comment to herself. It wouldn't help to flaunt that fact, but only solidify Day's favoritism accusation.

Day's lips pursed. "Fine. Keep in constant contact."

"Of course. Let's go." Taylor gestured to Elliott and Price before jogging after Wyatt, Levi and Shadow.

They caught up to them, and Taylor stepped in line with Wyatt. "You okay?"

Elliott flanked Shadow and Levi. Price brought up the rear. Protection all around.

"Fine. Just eager to get that phone and get out of the forest."

Wyatt kept his eyes on his son. "I wish I had his childlike faith, but I struggle with so many doubts."

"All Christians have doubts at times." Taylor sure did. "We can use those times to grow in Him."

"*Pfft*. You sound like my mother."

"Is that such a bad thing?" Taylor focused on Levi and Shadow while her trained eye checked her peripheral vision for any suspicious activity in the forest.

But so far, the woods remained silent. Thankfully.

Wyatt snatched a stick from the path and chucked it into the trees. "No, my mother is amazing. Dad, too, even though he's had bumpy relationships with his kids."

"I remember you telling me that. Do you get along with all your siblings?" Taylor was an only child and her relationship with her mother had been strained ever since Taylor's father walked out on them.

"Mostly. I'm the closest to Iris and also Tanner."

"You mentioned Iris lived in British Columbia. Where's Tanner?"

"Yukon. He's a search and rescue pilot."

"Cool." Taylor hit her radio button. "Day, any movement in your area?"

"Only squirrels and the occasional rabbit. You?" The constable's irritated tone sailed through the airwaves.

"Good. No, nothing here." Taylor prayed it would stay that way.

Thirty minutes later, the group climbed the incline after passing the caves and proceeded onto the path leading to the cliffs. She turned to Wyatt. "I didn't think Levi was this far up the mountain."

"Me neither. Hey, bud, why were you way up here? Didn't you hide the phone before you came this far?"

Levi spun around. "No, Papa. I told you. After the caves." He continued walking with Shadow and Elliott.

That definitely wasn't what Levi had said at the breakfast

table yesterday, and from Wyatt's knitted brows, he agreed. She leaned close. "Is Levi prone to lying?"

Wyatt stopped, his lips pursing. "Why would you ask that? I taught my son to always tell the truth no matter what the circumstance."

"I'm sorry, but it's not what he said earlier. Could he be confused?"

"Well, being kidnapped can certainly traumatize anyone, especially a five-year-old." Wyatt continued to follow his son, leaving his sarcasm lingering in the fresh air.

She'd struck a nerve.

Taylor quickened her pace to close the distance between them. "The cop in me had to ask. I'm sorry."

Wyatt remained silent.

Taylor exhaled slowly and hit her radio button. "Day, looks like we're heading toward Kesbush Gorge. Meet us there and keep alert."

No response.

"Samantha?" Taylor rarely called the constable by her given name, but her silence had Taylor concerned.

"I heard you. Copy."

Taylor's shoulders relaxed. All was fine. Except for the constable's hostility toward her, but that was just another normal day.

"Papa, it's here," Levi yelled.

Taylor and Wyatt rushed to his son's side.

Levi pointed to a hole in a tree close to the canyon trail.

"Don't touch it, Levi." Taylor put on her latex gloves and plucked the device from the hiding spot. "Good boy. You were smart to hide this."

Levi smiled. "I know."

Wyatt chuckled and tousled his son's curls. "You're just like your grandpa."

Movement rustled the bushes to their right.

Elliott's hand flew to his sidearm.

Day raised her hands. "Just us. Good, you found the phone. Pass it over. I'll take it to Forensics." She held out her gloved hand, wiggling her fingers.

Taylor complied. "Appreciate that." She glanced around Day. "Where are the others?"

"Cam got an important call from Supervisor Bain to return to their station. Ash went with him. They didn't want to leave, but I told them I'm a big girl and could take care of myself."

Of course you did.

Day placed the phone in her uniform vest pocket and tapped on it. "I'll keep it safe. There were no signs of any hunters. Maybe they're regrouping after their deal-gone-wrong the other day."

"Let's hope that's the case," Taylor said. "Radio me when you get back."

Day saluted Taylor and scrambled back through the forest.

Wyatt handed Levi a granola bar and approached the group. "Hux and Constable Elliott, can I tell you where I found those crates? It will probably take the both of you to carry it out. I want to get my son out of the forest and back to my ranch."

"That will leave only Taylor to protect you and not what Supervisor Mitchell wanted," Elliott said.

Taylor had to agree with Day for once. "I know, but Day is right. There have been no signs of the hunters. Plus, Wyatt is armed and trained in law enforcement."

Huxley squeezed Wyatt's shoulder. "Sure, bud. We'll take care of it. Where were they?"

Wyatt explained, giving clear details. The two men left.

"Is there a quicker route than the way we came?" Taylor asked.

Wyatt pointed to the right. "Through the canyon. I've taken Levi that way before, so he knows it well."

"I'll radio Bryan and give him the plan." Taylor explained the situation to her leader. He wasn't happy, but understood. "Let's go, Wyatt. Shadow, protect."

The dog returned to Levi's side as the group descended onto the canyon's trail.

After ten minutes of trekking on the rocky path, Shadow's ears flattened, and he growled, alerting the group to danger.

Taylor whipped out her weapon, searching for activity.

An explosion blasted behind them, followed by a tornado of rocks tumbling down the mountainside.

Barreling straight toward them.

TEN

Wyatt's head throbbed as a knot of terror lodged in his throat. He grasped his son around the waist, ignoring the lingering pain in his injured arm, and lifted him. "Taylor, run! Get to higher ground." Wyatt stumbled while dodging boulders raining down upon them. He nestled his son tighter in his arms and held his hand over top of Levi's head. Behind him, Shadow barked and Taylor yelled into her radio, requesting assistance and a chopper evacuation.

But would help arrive in time?

A bullet pinged off a rock in front of Wyatt, stopping him in his tracks. He examined the cliffs. Three hunters stood on the ridge, rifles pointed in their direction.

They were pinned down. Shooters above them, falling rocks below.

Lord, if You're listening, give us safe passage out of the park. Save my son!

Panic clawed at Wyatt, paralyzing his body as everything faded into a tunnel of chaos.

"Wyatt! Concentrate and fire back!"

Taylor's forceful tone snapped Wyatt out of his frozen state. He shielded Levi and pulled out his weapon. He fired toward the hunters, but his bullets went wide.

Another rock tumbled toward Taylor and she leaped out of the way, but fell to the ground.

"Taylor! You okay?"

She brushed the dust off her uniform and examined her radio. "My radio took the brunt of it." She hit the button. "It's broken. We have to hide, but where?"

Wyatt scanned the rugged terrain. The landslide stopped raining rocks, but a wall of debris now blocked their path. There would be no escape upward with the hunters pinning them down. "We have to go back into the canyon. Take refuge in the caves until help arrives." He spied a hiding spot and pointed. "Go there!"

They cowered behind a large boulder. Wyatt set Levi down. "Son, bring your knees to your chest and cover your head with your hands. Daddy needs to help Miss Taylor."

"Okay, Papa. I pray like Gramma." Levi did as instructed while he murmured prayers.

There was that childlike faith again. Wyatt Hoyt could learn from his five-year-old son.

Taylor reloaded her Glock. "Okay, where's the nearest cave?"

Wyatt pointed. "That way, but we can't outrun bullets. How long before help arrives?"

"Good question. I don't even know if my request for help went through. Wait, didn't you pack a sat phone?"

"Yes." His shaky fingers fumbled to unzip the front pocket. *Get it together.* Finally, he fished the device out and punched in the park warden's number.

"Price here."

"Hux. It's Wyatt. We need help in the Kesbush Canyon. Pinned down by hunters. Where are you?"

"Not far. We heard the explosion and turned around."

"Good. Taylor radioed for backup. Did that go through? You know what reception is like around here."

A brief silence followed while muffled voices sounded in the background. "Yes, Elliott confirmed that there's a chopper on the way. ETA fifteen to twenty minutes."

"We don't have that long. Trying to get to the cave to take refuge. Hunters are on the ridge east of our previous location."

Pffftttt. Another bullet pinged off the rock they hid behind as if confirming his predicament.

Wyatt ducked on instinct. *Come on!*

"We're almost to the ridge. Cam and Ash are on their way back, too. Hold tight and wait for us before heading to the cave." Hux's last words came out garbled. He was running.

"Copy." Wyatt punched off the call and stashed the phone into his pack's front pocket.

"Good news, I hope." Taylor fired another shot.

"Yes, the chopper is on the way and so are reinforcements. Hux and Elliott will return fire on the ridge."

Wyatt checked on his son. Shadow had nestled close beside the boy and Levi had his arm around the dog as if protecting each other.

Five minutes later, shouts echoed throughout the canyon, along with additional firepower. Wyatt glanced upward, shielding the sun from his eyes. The hunters were gone from the ridge.

"We must move now. Not sure how long before the shooters return." Wyatt hauled Levi up into his arms and turned to Taylor. "Ready?"

She nodded. "I'll cover you in case they're hiding. You keep Levi safe." She sprang out from behind the boulder and fired again. "Shadow, protect!"

Wyatt ran as fast as he could, sidestepping the landslide pile and heading toward the caves. He prayed for no bullets to reach them. He snuck a peek over his shoulder to check Taylor's position.

She crouch-walked, her gun steady and locked on the cliffs.

He cast another glance at the ridge.

The hunters had disappeared. Probably the added power of Hux and Elliott had scared them into retreating in the bush. Or they'd been apprehended.

Wyatt prayed it was the latter. They could use a break right about now.

He reached the cave. "Taylor, in here!" Wyatt crouched through the low entrance.

Taylor and Shadow followed.

Wyatt set Levi down and unclipped his flashlight, shining it around to ensure they were alone, but no animals greeted them. Thankfully. "We made it."

"Wyatt, those hunters were ready for us. How?"

"No idea. Who all knew we were coming here this morning?" Wyatt took out Levi's water bottle and handed it to him. "Drink up, bud. Help is coming." He inched back to where Taylor leaned against the cave's wall, her gun still raised as she guarded the entrance.

"Only us, our leaders, and those who helped search. Plus Dispatch." She cast her sight back onto Wyatt. "We have a mole among us."

Wyatt hissed out a breath. "I'm getting tired of this game Ridge is playing."

"I'm afraid he's only just started." She removed her binoculars from her backpack and pointed them toward the ridge.

"See anything?"

"No. Hunters are gone. I'm gonna step outside the entrance for a better look." She didn't wait for his response and left.

Wyatt held his breath, waiting for her return.

She reappeared after a few seconds. "The ridge appears to be clear, but I have a feeling those hunters aren't far away."

Wyatt approached and placed his hands on each of her arms. "You're not hit, are you?"

"No, but I'm as angry as a stirred-up hornet's nest. Someone has infiltrated our law enforcement, but whose? Yours? Or mine?"

"Could even be the park's. They were aware of the situation, but I trust Hux with my life."

Her forehead crinkled. "I'm not so sure we can trust anyone at this point." Her voice cracked.

Her earlier anger was elevating her emotions.

Wyatt brought her into an embrace, holding tightly. "It's gonna be okay. We'll get through this because I refuse to believe anything else." He willed that to be true.

Taylor drew back. "You always were such a positive person. I appreciate that about you. Sometimes my negative Nelly mother rubs off on me."

He wiped her escaped tear with his thumb, his gaze drifting to her lips. What would it be like to finally kiss her? Their brief two-month relationship ended abruptly before he got the chance. The moment he shared his heart, she retreated, and the kiss he'd dreamed of was lost. Forever.

Thankful that his son sat in the cave's shadows, Wyatt leaned closer until his lips were inches from hers.

She let out a soft cry and placed her hand on his chest. "Don't. I can't."

He stepped backward. "I'm sorry. Got caught up in the moment. You know that adrenaline-fueled emotional roller coaster?" What was he thinking? *You promised yourself.*

"It's okay, we—"

Shadow barked and shot out of the cave's entrance.

A woman's bloodcurdling scream echoed throughout the canyon like a boomerang on repeat.

Taylor withdrew her weapon and darted from their hiding spot.

Wyatt took out his gun but remained at the entrance. He would not abandon his son.

He adjusted the rim of his cowboy hat farther down to shield the glare from the beating sun, and caught a glimpse of an object lying a few feet from the cave.

A woman's body, but not a random hiker.

Constable Samantha Day.

A vise gripped Taylor's heart, tightening her chest as she squatted and pressed her fingers to her fellow constable's neck. No pulse. Not that she'd expected one. No way anyone could survive a plunge from that height. She searched for a glimpse of Day's killer, but the ridge remained silent.

Shadow let out a low-rumbled growl as movement sounded behind her. She bolted upright, whipping her gun toward whoever approached.

Warden Price raised his hands. "Just me." His eyes widened at the sight of the constable's body. "Is she—"

"Yes. Did you see anyone who might have pushed her?"

"No. Too busy helping Elliott apprehend a hunter. We never made it to the crates. I suspect they're gone now." Hux's gaze traveled across the area. "Where are Wyatt and Levi?"

"In the cave. I came out when I heard Sam scream." She holstered her gun. "Hunters gone?"

"For now. We caught one. Elliott is taking him to the station. The other two escaped. Disappeared. Not sure how."

"They seem to have a habit of doing that. It's almost like they found a hidden exit in the park."

"I doubt that. I'm not aware of any secret passageways." He harrumphed. "Then again, I didn't know about the retooled red bridge." Hux tipped his chin toward Day's body. "I thought she was on her way to the station to take that cell phone to Forensics."

Taylor sucked in a breath. "The phone!" She squatted and searched Day's pockets. "Ugh! It's gone." She hopped to her feet, anger burning her cheeks. "Ridge did this. He somehow realized we found it and killed her to get it back."

"Wait." Hux circled the constable's body and pointed to her face. "This was more than just a shove off the cliff. Look at the welt on her face and her swollen eye. She—"

"Was tortured." Taylor finished his statement, her shoulders drooping in remorse over the loss of her colleague.

Not that she and Constable Samantha Day were close. Far from it, but no one deserved this. She paid the price for a sick man's ruthless rise in his weapons-smuggling empire.

"There was obviously something on the phone Ridge killed

to keep buried from police and he must have beaten her to determine if she had seen any information on it." Hux squeezed her arm. "I'm sorry for your loss. Did you know her well?"

"Thanks. No, not really."

"Taylor, is it safe to come out?" Wyatt shouted from the cave's entrance.

"No! Stay there." Taylor failed to keep the trepidation from her voice, but she couldn't let Levi see the blood and mutilated body.

Once again, Shadow growled.

Taylor spun around to check what her K-9 alerted to.

Asher and Cam jogged toward them.

"You okay?" Cam's gaze diverted to Day's body, his jaw dropping. "What happened?"

"Someone pushed Constable Day from up there." Taylor pointed to the cliff. "I thought you guys returned to the station."

"Bain sent us back when he heard your radio message over the police scanner." Asher dropped by Day's side and took her hand. "No, my sweet Sam."

"Asher, please don't touch her body. We have to get the medical examiner here." Taylor hovered close to him. "Wait, you were dating her?"

He released her hand. "Yes. I was about to propose." Tears glistened in the man's eyes.

"I'm so sorry for your loss."

He rose and marched into Taylor's personal space. "Are you? She told me about the feud between the two of you. Maybe you killed her!"

Taylor stumbled backward at his brazen move.

Shadow growled and barked, repositioning himself in between Asher and Taylor.

"I did not. Now step away or you'll see what Shadow can do." Taylor kept her gaze fixed on the man.

"I'm sorry. I didn't mean that." His hushed words revealed the grief thrust upon him at his girlfriend's death. "Do you know what happened?"

"Dr. Oke will determine the cause of death, but it's obvious that she was beaten and pushed from the cliff." Taylor could never erase Day's bone-chilling scream from her memory. "Speaking of the medical examiner, I need to get Wyatt's sat phone to call in Dr. Oke and Forensics. My radio got hit in that rockslide. This is now an active crime scene." She pointed to the ridge. "As well as up there."

"I have one. Use mine, love." Cam fished the device out of his backpack and handed it to her.

She cringed at his term of endearment. *I am not your love, nor will I ever be.* His or anyone else's. Why did this man give her the heebie-jeebies? Was it because of the way he treated Wyatt or something different?

Taylor set aside her silent questions and punched in Bryan's number, distancing herself from the men. She wanted to keep her conversation private because right now she only trusted Wyatt and her sergeant.

"Sergeant Mitchell speaking."

"Bryan, it's Taylor. I wanted to update you on the situation here." Taylor shared the most recent events, including Day's death. "Sir, someone must pay. Sam was only doing her job."

"They will." His two words hissed through the phone, revealing his anger at his constable's senseless death. "I'll get the crime scene unit there as well as Dr. Oke. As I understand, the chopper should be there any moment. Get back to the ranch. Stat."

She didn't miss his angered tone morphing into one of concern for her. His fatherlike compassion was evident, and it warmed her heart. "We will. I'm struggling, Bryan." Taylor swallowed the kaleidoscope of emotions living in her throat.

"Sweet girl, remember that God's got you in His hands and He won't let go. And neither will I."

Taylor's knees buckled, her earlier adrenaline waning. "Thank you. I know God is with me. Just sometimes hard to see Him through my messy sea of doubts and storms of life."

"Understood, but remember we're safe with Him and He only wants us to step out in faith. I realize you've gone through trauma with losing Echo as well as what happened in Nova Scotia. Please don't let those circumstances define you or your amazing abilities. He gifted you. Use the tools He's given you and bring Ridge to justice."

Her gaze traveled from Day's body to the cave's entrance where Wyatt stood watching and waiting. Taylor marshaled strength into her legs, committing to stopping whoever killed Day and targeted Wyatt and Levi. "Thank you. I needed your pep talk."

The whirling of helicopter blades sounded in the distance.

"The chopper is coming. I gotta go."

"Stay safe. You said Huxley is there?"

"Yes." Taylor studied the warden. He appeared to be dependable, but could they trust him? Wyatt seemed to think so, but Taylor didn't know the man.

"Have him guard the crime scene, and I'll get a unit there ASAP, as well as the medical examiner."

"Copy. Chat later." She ended the call and returned to the group, handing Hux the phone. "Sergeant Mitchell requested you stay here until his team and the medical examiner arrive."

"I can do that."

The chopper's approach intensified, the rhythmic *thwup-thwup* of the blades thundering off the cliffs. The aircraft crested the ridge and dipped, hovering in search of the perfect landing spot. Brutal wind gusts blasted from the spinning rotors, pelting a storm of dust and loose rocks toward everything in its path.

Taylor shielded her face and jogged back to the cave. "Wyatt, time to go." She latched on to his arm, leaning close. "But don't let Levi see Sam's body. It's not pleasant."

"Understood." He approached Levi. "Bud, guess what? We're going for a helicopter ride. Would you like that?"

Levi hopped up. "Yes, Papa! Let's go." He skipped around Wyatt.

"Wait, son. I'll carry you." Wyatt scooped him up into his arms, holding his head close. "Keep your eyes shut because there's a lot of dust out there. Okay?"

"Yep."

Wyatt tipped his chin toward Taylor. "Ready."

She nodded. "Shadow, come."

The group bypassed the crime scene as they crouch-ran to the search and rescue chopper.

The door swung open and the SAR officer beckoned them forward. "Get in."

"Shadow, up," Taylor commanded.

The dog hopped inside and the trio followed, climbing into their seats before buckling in. They put on ear defenders to help deafen the noise and to communicate with the pilot.

"Ready," Taylor said into the mic.

The helicopter lifted, ascending with each shrill of excitement from Levi.

Taylor focused on Wyatt. "He's never been in a chopper before?"

"Nope. This is his first time." Wyatt messed up his son's curls.

The picture of Levi and his mother on Wyatt's mantel entered her mind. "I'm assuming he inherited his curls from Lisa. Not you."

"Correct." Wyatt's expression softened. "He's the spitting image of her."

"I don't know. He has your gorgeous green eyes."

He smiled his lopsided grin. "You think so?"

Oops. She hadn't meant to say that out loud.

She also hadn't counted on her feelings cropping up again, but they had.

Taylor couldn't deny it any longer.

She silenced a soft cry and gazed out the window as the ground below grew smaller. They reached the cliff's highest peak within moments.

A hunter appeared on the ridge, aiming a weapon in their direction.

Taylor pointed. "Machine gun!"

"I see him," the pilot yelled. "Compensating. Hold on!"

The chopper banked to the right.

Levi's earlier squeals turned to screams.

Shadow barked.

Taylor's breath hitched, and she forgot to breathe as she waited for the spray of bullets to pepper the chopper.

Lord, please save us!

ELEVEN

Wyatt clutched Levi's hand as the chopper righted itself and switched directions away from the shooter, moments before a bullet hit the tail. The helicopter swayed but remained level. Wyatt scanned the cliff to catch a glimpse of their attacker, but the image of the man grew smaller as they ascended and fled in an opposite trajectory.

"Bird's taken a hit. Executing emergency set-down." The pilot's voice hissed through the radio. "Spotted a clearing. One klick out. Hold tight—brace for impact." The pilot muttered his mayday and coordinates into the radio.

Wyatt turned to his whimpering son. "Levi, we're going to be okay. Remember what G'pa taught you when we flew together to Grandma's last year?"

Tears welled in the corner of his eyes as he nodded, then assumed the crash position.

"He's smart for such a young boy," the SAR officer said before bending over and placing his hands over his head.

"He is. Say a prayer, okay, bud?" Wyatt mimicked his son's movements and said his own prayer. *God, please hear me. Save us. Help the chopper land safely.*

It wasn't long before they reached the clearing and the chopper descended, swaying as the pilot maneuvered downward.

Moments later, the landing skids thumped onto the ground, jolting them in their seats.

"We're good, folks," the pilot said. "Help is on the way."

Levi clapped, his earlier screams vanishing. "Papa, God answered my prayer."

"He sure did, son." *Thank You.*

"Amen." Taylor unbuckled herself and dropped beside her dog, running her hands along his body.

"Is he okay?" Wyatt took off his ear defenders.

Shadow barked.

Taylor chuckled. "I guess that means yes. He didn't react when I examined him, so he's good."

"Time to get off and a safe distance away." The SAR officer slid open the side door and jumped from the chopper, holding out his hand. "Levi, you're next. I've got you."

Wyatt unfastened Levi's buckle. "Go, son."

The five-year-old reached for the officer's open arms, letting the man take him to safety.

Wyatt, Taylor and Shadow scrambled off the chopper, ensuring they were far enough away in case the aircraft exploded.

Taylor consulted with the pilot and officer on the chopper's condition.

Levi ran toward Wyatt and flew into him, hugging his legs. "Papa, that was close." He peered up at Wyatt with wide eyes. "Can we call G'pa and tell him I did what he said?"

Wyatt ruffled Levi's hair. "Of course, but let's wait until we get home, okay, bud?"

Levi stepped back and took his father's hand. "Let's go, Papa."

Taylor jogged over to them. "Pilot says the helicopter is salvageable, but we'll have to either hike from here or wait for crews to come on ATVs. Do you know how far we are from the park station?"

Wyatt wasn't sure he wanted to be in the wilderness with Levi for any longer than he had to. The hunters were still out there and seemed to have a constant eye on them. How? Ugh! He silenced his questions and pivoted in a sharp one-eighty, eyes sweeping the area to get his bearings. "It's about an hour and a half from here. How far out are the ATVs?"

"Pilot says their ETA is forty minutes."

"Beats an hour-and-a-half hike."

Roaring engines sounded in the distance.

Shadow barked.

Wyatt flinched, and his hand flew to his sidearm. That didn't add up to what Taylor just reported. Something was wrong. "Take cover. That may be the hunters returning."

Taylor withdrew her Glock. "Where?"

Wyatt cast his gaze around the clearing, spying a cluster of trees. "Get the others over there now." He lifted Levi into his arms. "Time to play hide-and-seek, son."

"Yippee!"

If only it was truly just a game.

Wyatt scurried toward the trees, Levi jostling in his arms. Pounding footfalls told him that the others were close behind. He focused on getting his son somewhere out of sight—and fast. He wouldn't let the hunters have another shot at hurting his son.

Would this mess ever end? *Lord, aren't You listening? Are You really there?*

Doubts plagued his mind, but he set them aside and pushed his jellylike legs to move faster. Almost there.

Wyatt quickly found a hiding spot and set Levi behind a fallen log. "Stay here, okay?"

"Yes, Papa. I'll count to twenty."

Wyatt smiled. "Perfect. I'm gonna be over there." He pointed to an aspen beside him. He leaned against the tree trunk, withdrawing his weapon.

Taylor hid beside the tree to his right. "Shadow, protect." She gestured toward Levi.

Shadow zipped over to Levi's side, nestling close.

The others each hid nearby.

The engine roars grew louder.

Wyatt white-knuckled his 9mm and peeked around the tree, scouring the clearing.

Two ATVs stopped near the damaged helicopter. The riders

removed their helmets and dismounted. They turned in their direction.

Cam Field and Asher Calloway.

Relief flooded Wyatt's limbs. "We're good. It's only Field and Calloway." He sheathed his gun.

"Wait, Wyatt. How did they get here so fast? They were just with us in the canyon." Taylor's elevated pitch revealed her angst.

"Good question." Could one or the other be involved somehow? Suspicion niggled at him, but he quickly dismissed the idea. Sure, Field was annoying, but a killer? No. And Wyatt had known Calloway for years. He was a trusted park guide and everyone loved the easygoing man.

Then again, right now, he didn't trust anyone. "Let's find out, shall we?" He motioned to the SAR officer. "Stay here with my son, okay?"

"Sure." He motioned toward the pilot. "We both will, but be careful."

"I'll whistle when it's safe to come out." Taylor stepped out from behind the tree, but kept her Glock in a ready position, pointing downward and close to her waist. "Wyatt, we do this together." She faced her K-9. "Shadow, stay."

Wyatt brought out his 9mm again and followed Taylor into the clearing.

"Police. Show your hands," Taylor yelled.

Field and Calloway turned at her command.

"It's only us." Field raised his hands.

Asher did the same.

Taylor and Wyatt reached the pair within seconds.

"How did you get here so quickly?" Taylor asked, holstering her weapon.

Wyatt did the same, but kept his hand on his 9mm. "You were just in the canyon with us."

Field glared at Wyatt. "Cowboy, simmer down. A couple park

employees came to the canyon and we borrowed their ATVs. We took the Foxwick Trail. You know the one."

Calloway pushed his long bangs out of his eyes. "We heard the shots and saw the chopper get hit, so we left Hux and the others behind and raced here."

"Good thing we did, too." Field pointed to the downed chopper. "You need help getting back to the station. Where's Levi?"

"Safe." Wyatt was aware of the trail Field referred to, but something still didn't sit well with him.

Or was his imagination playing havoc? Hux's warning about Field flashed through his mind. He marched into the man's personal space. "Why did you tell Hux that I had this coming? Are you part of the smuggling ring?"

"How can you even ask that?" Field crossed his arms, his nostrils twitching. "I just meant that you let that boy run wild in the forest too much. This was bound to happen. You know how criminals take advantage of young kids."

"What are you talking about? Someone is always with Levi." Anger flushed Wyatt's cheeks and he counted to five slowly to subdue his emotions.

"That's enough," Calloway said. "We have more pressing matters going on. Anyone hurt?"

"No, thankfully." Taylor gestured toward the ATVs. "You okay if we take your vehicles? We need to get Levi out of the forest. I'm guessing the hunters are close by and the park employees are still thirty minutes out."

"For you, sweetheart, of course." Field winked, his sly tone clear.

Wyatt's stomach soured at the man's words. After all, Field had a girlfriend. How could he be so flippant toward women?

Taylor's face tightened. "While I appreciate you giving us your ATVs, I'm not your sweetheart—and never will be."

Good for you. At least one woman saw through the handsome smooth talker.

"Time to go." Taylor placed two fingers into her mouth and whistled. Her cue for the others to come.

Shadow barked in the distance before emerging from the tree line, with the others close behind.

After commandeering the two-seater ATVs and updating their leaders at the park station, Wyatt lifted a tired Levi and followed Taylor into his ranch two hours later.

Wyatt's cell phone rang, and he set Levi down. "Son, go into the den and grab a book. I'll come and read to you, okay, bud?" He addressed Taylor. "Maybe Miss Taylor could make us some PB&J sandwiches?"

She laughed. "Of course."

"Yay!" Levi scampered down the hallway.

Wyatt fished his phone from his pocket, reading the screen. Unknown Caller. He hovered over the button before hitting Answer. "Hoyt here."

"Good job getting Levi out of the forest," the robotic voice said.

Wyatt hitched in a breath. Not again. "Who's this?"

"Someone you'd never guess. I almost had you both. Don't think you're safe. I will find you." *Click.*

Dread lodged in Wyatt's stomach, twisting like a knife. He locked his door, slamming the dead bolt into place before setting his alarm to the stay position. If anyone tried to enter, the alarm would sound.

But would all the safety provisions protect them from a madman determined to take them out?

Taylor extracted a butter knife from the utensil drawer with her shaky fingers and took several cleansing breaths to calm her shattered nerves. The latest threat from Ridge had sent both her and Wyatt into a panic-stricken state. His lighthearted expression switched to one of terror as he spoke on the phone. Taylor had immediately called her sergeant to explain the situation. He promised to ramp up patrol over Wyatt's property. But would that be enough to stop Ridge from terrorizing them with his violent bullying? *Lord, please silence the storms raging through Wyatt. I can see them brewing in his eyes. Keep Levi safe. Don't let Wyatt lose him, too.*

Levi's giggles erupted from the living room.

Taylor grinned. At least the five-year-old's playful personality could make them forget their predicament. For a minute or two. She stuck her knife into the peanut butter and slapped it onto the bread, taking her fears out one slather at a time.

She had checked her inbox and discovered a response from the retired constable, stating that he'd be open to a video call. She set up an appointment in an hour. Would the man be able to provide any answers?

The pitter-patter of feet sounded on the hallway hardwood floor, interrupting her thoughts.

Seconds later, Levi burst into the room. "PB&J s'miches ready, Miss Taylor?"

Wyatt trudged in behind his son. "Don't rush her, Levi. You know sandwich-building takes time and we want to do it right." He grinned at Taylor and winked.

Her heart stuttered, sending butterflies fluttering. *Stop with that smile I love.*

She snatched a spoon from the drawer, keeping her attention on the bread. "Exactly, but they're almost ready." Taylor spooned the jam onto the opposite slices before putting them together.

Levi bounced on his heels. "We're gonna call G'pa now!"

Wyatt punched in the number on the cordless landline receiver. "I'm putting it on speaker. Hop up onto the island stool, son."

Levi obeyed.

"Hoyt residence," a male voice said.

"G'pa! Guess what?" Levi's excited tone blared in the room.

A chuckle sailed through the speaker. "Wait. Who am I speaking with?"

Levi rolled his eyes. "You're silly. It's me, Levi, G'pa."

"I know. What news do you have, Champ?"

"I did what you taught me to do on a plane."

Silence. "You mean the crash position?"

"Yes, G'pa! I did it on the chopper. Just like you said."

"Proud of you, Champ." Frank cleared his throat. "Wyatt, what happened?"

"Levi, why don't you take this to the dining room?" Taylor passed Levi plastic plates, diverting the boy out of the kitchen. "I'll bring in the sandwiches in a second."

The boy nodded. "Bye, G'pa. Time for s'miches. Love you." He held the stack of plates high as he shuffled toward the adjoining dining room.

"You, too, Champ." Frank paused before continuing, "Is that the constable you mentioned when you called earlier?"

"Yes, Constable Taylor Grant. She and Shadow are staying with us for our protection." Wyatt took Levi's stool, leaned closer to the phone's speaker, and explained the situation. "This smuggler Ridge is after us."

An audible sharp intake of breath filtered through the landline. "Why does trouble always find our family?"

"Good question." Wyatt's eyebrows drew tight, a furrow carving between them. "We went into the park to retrieve the phone Levi hid. He—"

"Wait. You purposely took my grandson back into the forest with a killer on the loose?" The man's tone changed to anger.

Wyatt raked his fingers through his hair. "I had to. We were running out of time."

His father hissed out a breath.

Taylor had to intervene. "Mr. Hoyt, we were well protected by other constables."

"Dad, let me explain." Wyatt shared the events of the day, including the helicopter's rough landing.

She noted he left out some details. Details a grandfather didn't need to know, especially with all the havoc the man had gone through recently.

"Thank the good Lord you're all safe. He was definitely looking out after you. Any updates on the case, Taylor? That you can tell me, of course."

"We apprehended a suspect today. Constables are questioning him now. I have another lead I'm following up on." She kept her response vague. Enough to satisfy him, but not too much to cross the line.

"Good to hear. Praying your department will find answers."

Wyatt pushed off the stool. "We gotta run. Levi just wanted to tell you about the chopper ride."

Tapping sounded over the line. "Do you need me to come to Newfoundland? I can look after Levi for you."

Wyatt rubbed his stubbled chin. "We're good. Taylor's leader has cruisers patrolling the ranch. I've locked the gate, too."

"Stay there and let the constables do their jobs."

Taylor cringed at the man's forceful command. Wyatt had told her all about Frank Hoyt but also that he'd softened over the past couple of years.

Wyatt pinched his lips together, his obvious frustration emerging for a split second before disappearing. "Talk to you later, Dad." His finger hovered over the off button on his landline. "Love you."

"You, too. Your mom and I will be on our knees. Keep me updated."

"Will do." Wyatt hit the button before seething a breath through his teeth. "I love him, but sometimes his old nature returns."

"He's just concerned for you and Levi." She cut the sandwiches and placed them on a plate. "At least you have a father who cares."

Wyatt opened the fridge and brought out water bottles. "Sorry. You never hear from yours?"

"Nope. Not since he walked out on us when I was six." An image of Taylor sitting on her father's knee as he read to her popped into her mind. She had loved the man dearly, following him around like a lost puppy. *Why did you leave, Daddy?*

It was a question Taylor had asked her mother repeatedly for months and years after his disappearance, but her mother never had an answer. She had even contacted the police, but no one could track the man down. It was like he vanished. Her mother had changed after that. Became withdrawn. Not that Taylor blamed her. Terri Grant had taken two jobs just to make ends meet. She no longer had time to raise her daughter. Taylor quickly became independent.

Today, their fragile mother-daughter relationship sat heavy on Taylor's chest, impossible to ignore. Their conversations were sparse, similar to those one would have with an acquaintance. Sure, Taylor longed for a deeper relationship, but her mother became too bitter to be around.

Taylor tried to bridge the gap. However, her mother lived in the past and couldn't move on. And now, her mother recently dropped the bombshell that she had indeed spoken to Taylor's father throughout the years, but kept that a secret. In her mother's words she "hesitated to make Taylor's pain worse." It was clear Ken Grant didn't want to have anything to do with them, especially his own daughter.

Get her out of your head. "Let's eat, shall we?" She didn't wait for a response, but headed to the dining room.

An hour later, Wyatt and Taylor sat at the dining room table while Levi watched cartoons.

Time to get some answers. *Please Lord, make it happen.*

"Thanks for taking my call, Mr. Atkins." She gestured toward Wyatt. "This is Conservation Officer Wyatt Hoyt."

"Nice to meet you both. Please call me Fred." The retired constable leaned into his computer's camera, giving Taylor and Wyatt an enlarged view of his forehead. "Oops. Sorry. That was a little too close, huh?" He shifted backward, his full face appearing on the screen.

Taylor resisted the urge to giggle. "No problem. We were wondering if you could give us information on a cold case from four years ago."

He scratched his head. "Can you give me a bit more information? My memory isn't the best these days, and I worked on a lot of cold cases."

Wyatt inched closer to Taylor. "Sir, I'm not sure you remember me, but we met at the Kesbush Gorge when I reported two men smuggling cases across the red bridge."

Fred's eyes brightened in recognition. "Oh yes. I thought you looked familiar. You were just new to the job, right?"

"Yes. We—"

Taylor's cell phone rang. Sergeant Mitchell. She had told him about their video call, so if he was reaching out now, it was important. "I'm sorry. I have to take this. Be right back." She rose and exited the dining room, hitting Answer. "Sir, what's going on? We're talking to Fred."

"That's why I'm calling. Dr. Oke just called with the identification of the deceased male. Took her a bit as the man tried to erase his identity from our systems four years ago."

Taylor bristled. Four years. *That can't be a coincidence.* "Who is it?"

"Pete Atkins—Fred's nephew."

She drew in a sharp breath. "What? Do you think Fred left something out of his report to protect his nephew?"

"It's possible, but Fred was meticulous and by the book. Plus, we don't know if Pete was a buyer back then. He might not have been part of the smuggling ring. This could simply be a coincidence."

"Do you really think that? Because I don't."

Bryan sighed. "I'm hoping Fred didn't know about Pete. I worked with Fred. He's a good man."

"Well, I'm going to find out."

"Tread lightly. Fred is territorial when it comes to family."

"Anything on the hunter Elliott is questioning?" Taylor peeked into the family room to check on Levi. She smiled.

Shadow and Levi snuggled on the couch. Cartoons blaring, but they were both asleep.

Longing for a relationship with this family tugged at Taylor's heart. If only—

She retreated from the scene, pursing her lips. *Don't go there.*

"Elliott was waylaid. We had an influx of arrests this morning. He's with him now. I'll call you when I find out."

"Sounds good. Thanks for telling me about Pete."

"Thought you might want that info for your conversation. Chat later." He clicked off the call.

Taylor marched back into the dining room and plunked onto her chair, interrupting the men's conversation. "Fred, is your nephew involved with this smuggling ring?"

The man's lips pinched into a tight line.

Wyatt's head tilted, his eyes flashing a silent question.

"What are you talking about, young lady?" The man's former sweet demeanor morphed into one of contempt.

So much for treading lightly.

Wyatt's gaze shifted back to the retired constable with a question plunging through his head. What had Taylor's leader told her in their two-minute phone call?

Taylor opened her mouth and closed it again, as if gathering her thoughts. She paused before continuing. "I'm sorry to tell you this, Fred, but our prime suspect killed your nephew in a case involving the potential same ring as four years ago."

What? "Dr. Oke confirmed the identity?" Wyatt asked.

"Yes, but it took longer than normal. Seems Pete Atkins tried to erase his identity." She steepled her fingers and leaned into the screen. "An odd coincidence, don't you think, Fred? Especially because you were assigned that case. Did you know about your nephew's involvement with the ring?"

"No!" Fred averted his gaze to something—or someone—off-screen.

What was he hiding?

Wyatt had to appeal to the man's conscience. "Sir, I'm sorry for your loss, but my five-year-old son's life is at stake here. Anything you can tell us about Pete's involvement would help. Did you discover evidence that you didn't include in your report four years ago?"

"It's time, Fred." A woman's voice sounded off-screen. "We can no longer deny Pete's illegal activities."

Fred's gaze returned to the camera, his shoulders slumping. "Wyatt, you were wrong about one thing all those years ago. There weren't two men, but three. When I crossed the bridge, I noted someone fleeing into the woods."

"Pete." How had Wyatt missed another person? Sure, he was a rookie back then, but always prided himself on being observant. His father taught him that. "Why didn't you follow and arrest him?"

"I tried, but he disappeared and I honestly wasn't sure it was him. I only caught a glimpse. Until..." His voice trailed off.

"Until what, Fred?" Taylor asked. "Anything you can tell us may help. Someone killed your nephew. Don't you want justice, even if he was involved? We must stop this ring, sir."

He hissed out an elongated breath. "Until I found a map of the park in Pete's backpack with what I assumed were marked locations and smuggling routes. He stayed with me at the time, and when I confronted him, he said it was only a treasure-hunt game he played with his buddies. He denied he was at the red bridge that day. I believed him." He leaned into the camera. "He was a good kid but must have gotten in with a wrong crowd after I left Kesbush Bay."

"Has he been to visit you and your sister?" Wyatt asked.

"Only occasionally, and honestly, he seemed to thrive in his role as a janitor at a local high school and appeared to be happy." His voice broke. "And now we'll have to prepare for his funeral."

"Our deepest sympathies." While Wyatt ached for the man's loss, he surmised that Pete's uncle and mother didn't really know the person he'd obviously become.

Taylor picked up her pen and clicked it multiple times. "Fred, is there anything else you can tell us about your investigation into the weapon-smuggling ring?"

"Only what's in my report."

Yeah, the report that was deleted. Wyatt kept that statement to himself. Wait— "What about the map? Did you give it back to Pete?"

The man's eyes brightened. "When I found it, I took a picture and printed it. I'm old-school regarding paperwork and thought it would be evidence, so I was going to log it, but then Pete explained about the game. I think I still have it packed in a box. If I find it, I'll take a picture and email it to you."

"Thank you, Fred. If there's anything else you can think of, let me know. Nice meeting you." Taylor's phone rang. "And I am truly sorry for your loss."

"Thank you. Bye." The man's face disappeared from the screen.

Taylor tapped End and checked her screen. "That's Bryan." She answered and put him on speaker phone. "Sir, I'm here with Wyatt. We just got off the call with Fred. What do you have?"

"Elliott informed me that the hunter gave him the date of when that huge weapon deal was going down."

Finally. A concrete lead.

Wyatt straightened in his seat, his PB&J sandwich turned to lead in his stomach at the idea of the upcoming danger.

Taylor gripped the sides of the table. "When, sir?"

"Day after tomorrow. Midnight. Due to the leak, we're keeping this on a need-to-know basis. We need you and Shadow there. You, too, Wyatt. You're more familiar with the area than we are."

"Understood." Wyatt would bring in the only other person he trusted to watch Levi. Frank Hoyt.

The sergeant gave the details of the plan to take down Ridge and his band of hunters.

Foreboding tightened Wyatt's chest.

Were they close to apprehending this ring? Or would this ruthless gang catch wind of the plan and slip through their fingers?

Again.

TWELVE

Two days later, Taylor edged her head around the entrance to the cave, every muscle taut. Her night-vision goggles illuminated the Kesbush Gorge in a creepy green wash, every shadow sharpened as she scanned the landscape, alert for the smallest movement. She and Wyatt huddled close with Shadow flanking them. The rest of the team, consisting of her sergeant, Constable Elliott and Warden Price, hid in strategic places surrounding the gorge. Her sergeant had kept the team to only a few, stating he didn't know who to trust. Small but mighty. At least, that's what she prayed for as they drove to Teragoose National Park.

Wyatt's father arrived in Kesbush Bay from Alberta yesterday and surprised his grandson. Levi was elated to see Frank Hoyt even though he didn't know the entire reason his grandfather had come. The protective man promised he'd stay awake and alert, on guard while the team took down this dangerous ring.

Please make that happen, Lord. We need this to be over.

It was now eleven forty-five, and the team was in place and heavily armed. Taylor had updated her sergeant on their conversation with the retired constable. Fred had emailed to report that he was still looking for the map, but Taylor guessed that he'd probably thrown it out. Why would he have kept it if he believed his nephew's claim of it being a treasure map?

Taylor removed her goggles and eyed Shadow. Her K-9 was equipped with a camouflaged Kevlar vest. She had it made to fit her dog perfectly. She wouldn't risk another K-9. Taylor hugged him. "God, protect Shadow," she whispered. "Don't let what happened to Echo happen to him."

Shadow nuzzled into his handler.

"What do you mean, Taylor? What happened to Echo?" Wyatt kept his voice low. "You haven't talked about him."

She cringed. She hadn't meant for him to hear her prayer. Her guilt over Echo's death had kept her from telling many about the incident.

Taylor released a soft breath. "Echo was my first K-9 in my rookie days." She moved closer to Wyatt, keeping her voice down. They were far enough away from the pulley system not to be heard, but she wasn't taking any chances of exposing their presence. "He was tracking a kidnapped hiker when he suddenly stopped and tugged on his leash to go left, but it wasn't the trail where the hiker was last seen."

"Why did he want to veer off the path?"

"Because he sensed the danger ahead, but I didn't trust him." She gripped Shadow's leash tighter, as if that would erase the memory of the mistake that cost Echo's life. "I held him back, and we forged on the current path. We were ambushed seconds later. The kidnapper aimed his gun at me, and Echo tore away from my hold. He broke his leash and launched into the air like a secret service agent protecting the president in the movies."

"He took the bullet for you."

"Yes." Taylor bit back threatening tears. "That's why I now have this special Kevlar vest for Shadow."

"I don't blame you. That must have been tough to go through. It wasn't only a loss of a family pet, but a partner." Wyatt squeezed her hand. "I'm so sorry."

"I still get teary-eyed thinking about Echo. He was such a good dog." She petted Shadow. "You are, too, boy."

"Why don't you talk about Echo?"

Taylor bit her lip. "Because I'm ashamed of myself. I should have trusted in his abilities, but I second-guessed why he tried to lead us away from the hiker's known location."

"We all make mistakes. Remember mine from four years ago? Right here at this exact location."

"I will never ignore my K-9's keen senses again." Her words seethed with anger. "It's why I try to control my situations now. I felt so powerless after."

"That's a valid fear, but we can't always control what happens. Isn't that what God's for?"

Ouch. Wise words from someone who says he doesn't believe. "You're right, but fears are real and sometimes even Christians forget to trust in the One who can deliver us from them." *Forgive me, Father.*

"True."

"Don't you have a fear that you find hard to shake?"

He jerked backward.

Taylor caught his sudden reaction to her question, even in the dark. "You can trust me, Wyatt. You know that, right?"

"I know. It's just hard to talk about." He puffed out a breath. "I failed my little brother and find it hard to forgive myself even after all these years."

"Why, what happened?"

"I rarely talk about Kyle, so that's why I didn't mention him when we dated. Tough subject." He shifted his position. "Kyle was bullied in school. We tried to stop it, but were unsuccessful."

"I hate bullies."

"They're cowards. Anyway, I tried to look out for him, but he kept saying he handled it. Months went by and he never complained about the boys, so I thought it had stopped." A pause. "Then one day I overheard him talking to some buddies, asking what the easiest way was to end it all. I was shocked and confronted him."

Taylor grabbed his arm. "What did he say?"

"That he was only joking around and not to worry. I believed him, but after my football practice ended, I hurried home to make sure he was okay." His voice quivered. "I was too late. He hung himself."

Taylor gasped, her heart going out to Wyatt. "I'm so sorry,

but that's not your fault. You know you couldn't have prevented it even if you did get home on time. If he was that determined, he would have tried again."

"That's what Mom said, but I just can't shake the guilt, and now it's escalated into a fear of failure." He hung his head. "I failed Kyle. Failed Lisa. I cannot fail my son, too."

Taylor brought him into a hug. "You won't. We'll get through this."

Wyatt wrapped his arms around her and clung tightly.

Shadow headbutted the duo, adding his emotional support.

Taylor could stay in his arms forever, but now wasn't the time for her emerging feelings to overshadow her job.

Protect the man before her and catch a killer.

She swallowed the lump in her throat and pulled back. "And for the record, you didn't fail either Kyle or Lisa. Please get that out of your head." She tapped on his right temple.

"You need to take your own advice. Stop blaming yourself for Echo's death. Yes, it was hard to lose him, but protecting you was his job."

"I keep telling myself that, but that night continues to plague my dreams." She shivered not only from the dampness, but from the eerie wave of terror running through her iced veins. "In fact, it was a similar night to this one. I think that's why it came pummeling back."

Wyatt hit his watch face, the screen illuminating the darkened cave. "It's now past midnight. Any sign of them?"

Taylor put her goggles back on and scanned the area outside the cave.

A foreboding silence blanketed the forest.

Not good.

She whispered into her radio, "Sergeant, anything on your end? All is quiet here."

"Same," he replied. "Stay vigilant. They're out there. I can feel it."

"Copy that." Taylor ducked back into the cave. "Where are they?"

"Did they catch wind of our takedown?"

Taylor took off her goggles, hating how they pinched the bridge of her nose. "How? Bryan kept this all on a need-to-know basis." She massaged her forehead.

Her radio crackled before her sergeant's voice came across the airwaves. "I scouted the area. Still nothing. We'll give it another hour."

"I don't like it, sir," Taylor responded.

"Agreed. Stay alert."

"Copy that." Taylor hunkered down in the cave. She hated waiting, but right now, she didn't have a choice.

Forty-five minutes later, Shadow let out a low rumbled growl.

The hairs at the back of her neck prickled, her breath constricting. Something—or someone—was out there.

A bone-chilling scream pierced the night.

Multiple shudders locked her already tense limbs.

Shadow bolted, straining against the leash.

Taylor held on to him. She would not let her dog loose.

Wyatt stiffened. Had the hunters captured a woman in one of their hidden traps? If so, they had to help her. "We have to find out where that scream came from."

"Agreed. Someone is in trouble." Taylor pressed her radio button. "Sergeant, did you hear that?"

"Yes. Sounded closer to your location."

Taylor pushed herself upright. "We'll check it out. Sir, I don't think the meet is happening. Did the prisoner give us bad intel?"

"Possibly. Or, like we suspected, somehow they caught wind of our takedown."

"But how?" Taylor asked. "Sir, is it possible the station is bugged?"

"I did a thorough sweep. It's clean."

Wyatt stuffed his hands in his pockets and fingered his cell phone, tensing. "There could be another possibility."

"What?" Taylor brushed dirt off her pants with her free hand. She pushed the radio button and held it toward Wyatt.

"Sir, they may have cloned one or more of our phones. We've been communicating through texts." Wyatt realized this wasn't a television show, but could it be possible?

"Good point, Wyatt. They may also be listening in on our channel somehow. Switch to our secret one, Taylor."

Another scream ripped through the night's shadows, terror clawing at Wyatt's chest. "We have to find where that's coming from."

"Agreed." Taylor fiddled with her radio. "Done. We're going to investigate the screams, sir."

"Be careful," Sergeant Mitchell ordered. "It may be a trap."

"Copy." Taylor put on her goggles and unleashed her Glock.

Wyatt did the same.

Taylor held on to Shadow's leash. "Let's go. Stay close."

"You realize I'm trained in law enforcement, right?" Why did her command irritate him so much?

"Yes. Sorry." She eased out from the cave in a crouch-walk, raising her weapon.

Get a grip, Wyatt. She's only doing her job and protecting you. He was tired. Tired of skulking through the forest, hunting for this ring. Tired of his foul attitude lately. And most of all—

Tired of the losses in his life. Kyle, Lisa, Denise, and the attempts on his son.

This has to end. Now.

Wyatt gathered strength and courage, gripped his gun tighter, and crept in behind Taylor.

Another scream echoed throughout the region.

Shadow barked, dragging Taylor toward the sound.

Trusting the dog's instincts, they let him lead them.

Seconds later, several eyes glistened through the eerie green hue of Wyatt's night-vision goggles. Relief relaxed his tense muscles. "I should have known. Red foxes make horrific cries that can sound like screams."

Shadow barked ferociously.

The foxes scattered into the forest, retreating from their presence.

Taylor sheathed her weapon. "I've seen a red fox, but never heard them scream like that. Weird."

"Yep. It's obvious the hunters aren't coming. We should probably head back to the ranch." Wyatt's weary body required rest and he wanted to check on Levi.

"Let me update Bryan." She spoke into her radio. "Sir, those screams were only red foxes. They retreated."

"That's a relief."

"We're going to return to the ranch now," Taylor said. "Clearly, the hunters changed their meet."

"Agreed. We'll wait another half hour before dispersing. Let me know when you're at the ranch."

"Copy. Keep me updated." Taylor shifted her position and faced Wyatt. "What's the best trail out of here?"

He pointed. "This way. I could get used to these goggles at nighttime. They would be useful."

Taylor chuckled. "Well, I doubt Bryan will let you keep them."

"Listen, I'm sorry for my earlier comment. I know you trust my abilities." He emitted a wheezed breath. "Truth be told, it's my fear of failure taking over. I don't trust myself."

"Your record speaks for itself. Sure, you didn't catch this ring years ago, but you have helped stop countless illegal activities across Newfoundland and Labrador."

Had she been following his career these past couple of years? "You've been reading the headlines?"

"Hey, even though I moved for a few years, this is still my home."

Wyatt had been involved with a few takedowns of illegal

poachers and hunters, and lots of fishing citations. "I'm not a hero. Only doing my job."

"You are in my books. Keeping—"

Shadow barked.

A shot echoed to their left.

Wyatt pivoted.

A hunter stood in the distance, directly in their path.

"Take cover!" Wyatt shoved her to the right. "This way."

They scrambled onto the trail in the opposite direction of the hunter.

Another shot ripped through the darkness. This time to the right as an additional hunter appeared, blocking their route.

"They're herding us again!" Taylor fired at the shooter.

Wyatt flinched. The dangerous labyrinth of fallen trees was their only way around them now, and he'd gotten lost among the logs a few times. He had avoided the path—

But it was now their only way to safety.

THIRTEEN

Taylor didn't miss the alarm on Wyatt's face through her night-vision goggles. Beside her, Shadow continued to bark. A fresh surge of panic rippled throughout Taylor's muscles. She realized he was trying to tell her to release him, but could she trust he wouldn't get hurt like Echo? These hunters were dangerous. "Wyatt, how do we escape? Is there another way around these men?"

"Unfortunately, only one." His forced reply held trepidation.

"What is it?"

"There's a path directly in front of us." Wyatt remained frozen in place.

Another shot shattered the forest's silence.

"We have to go! What aren't you telling me?"

"It's dangerous and many hikers, including myself, have gotten lost in a maze of fallen trees and bushes." A breath hissed through his teeth. "And that's exactly where they're herding us toward."

"What could be worse than one of their bullets?"

"There are multiple places for hunters to hide in that section of the wilderness, lying in wait to ambush us." He tapped his chin. "That's what they're obviously wanting us to do. Your intel was wrong. This wasn't a smuggling deal. It was a trap to eliminate us."

He was right, and they fell for it. "We don't have a choice."

She noted his pinched expression.

"Taylor, we heard shots. You okay?" Her sergeant's concerned voice crackled through the radio.

"We're good, but taking a different route out of the forest," she replied. "Watch out for the hunters. They may be heading toward you. Sir, that prisoner led us astray. These hunters weren't setting up a buy. They brought us here to eliminate us."

"We're heading your way."

"No, sir. Get out of the forest. Now!" Taylor wasn't about to put the rest of the team at risk. Obviously, these hunters were after her, Wyatt and Shadow. But she wouldn't give them an easy target.

"Please stay safe."

"You, too, sir." Taylor turned to Wyatt. "Lead the way."

His lips pursed before he pivoted and dashed through a cluster of trees onto a rocky path filled with devastation.

Even in the darkness, a clear picture of the area came into focus through her goggles.

Multiple blackened trees stripped of their foliage from a forest fire blanketed the area, some still standing while others had collapsed to the ground, leaving enormous trunks in their path. Among the destruction, new trees had grown tall, but strong winds had knocked many on their sides.

The two destructive forces had turned the once vibrant part of the forest into a maze.

"Wyatt, when did this all happen?"

"The forest fire was over twenty-five years ago, but a hurricane whipped through here shortly after you moved."

Two years ago. "So what we have is a complex tangle of dead trees among fallen logs, creating a maze. Why didn't the park cut down all the dead trees?"

"Environmentalists refused to let them, but as you can see, new life quickly returned."

Even in the darkened hour, the scene would have been beautiful and a kid's fun playground if it wasn't for the hunters hot on their trail.

Shadow growled, reminding her that those men were close.

"We have to go, but which way?" She scanned the options through her goggles.

"It's been a while since I've been here, and the last time I got lost." He hesitated before rushing to the left. "This way." He sidestepped a fallen log and ducked between two new trees.

"Shadow, come." Taylor yanked on his leash and followed Wyatt.

Moments later, they reached a dead end, two uprooted trees with their massive exposed roots lying sprawled across the trail among the dense brush, blocking their path.

Not good.

"We have to retrace our steps and go the other way." Taylor pivoted and trudged back down the path, not waiting for Wyatt to respond.

An arrow lodged into the fallen tree to her right.

She screamed and fell to the ground, taking refuge behind a charred log.

"Taylor! You hit?" Wyatt dropped beside her, unleashing his weapon.

"No, but the arrow came close." Her heart rate increased, plummeting her into a full-fledged panic mode.

"Breathe, Taylor." Wyatt edged upward and stole a look over the log. "I don't see anyone."

Shadow growled, tugging on her leash.

"How will we get out of here?" She inhaled, exhaling slowly.

"This is why I didn't want to come this way."

Shadow barked and lunged forward a second time.

"Shadow sure wants to go somewhere," Wyatt whispered. "Is he telling you something?"

Lord, show me what to do? I can't lose another dog.

Set him free. The words launched into her mind, but her heart refused to listen. Was that what she was supposed to do? What if she misread the situation, and another ambush awaited them? Had Shadow found a different way out of this deadly labyrinth?

Set him free.

Taylor closed her eyes as if that would silence her mind. Could she let him go?

Shadow lunged again.

She had to. It was the only answer. She couldn't make the same mistake.

I need to trust in Shadow's abilities.

Taylor unhooked the leash from his collar. Shadow was trained in search and rescue. Only this time, his search would be for a way out of the wilderness. "Shadow, seek!"

The dog pivoted and barreled around the fallen log, heading toward the dead end.

"Where's he going?" Wyatt asked. "We just came from there. It's blocked."

"We have to trust him. There must be another way out." Taylor sprinted after Shadow, keeping low to the ground.

The heavy thud of footsteps behind her revealed Wyatt had followed.

Moments later, they reached the blocked path.

Shadow glanced over his shoulder at them and barked before plowing through the rotten roots.

"There's a hole." Taylor had failed to see it in the darkened night, but Shadow knew it was there. "Come on."

She raced toward it and dropped to her knees. She parted some roots and crawled through.

Dirt sprinkled on top of her, gritty against her exposed skin, but she ignored the thought of crawling insects writhing in the soil and pressed forward, focusing on their path to freedom.

Freedom from the deadly bandits behind them.

They reached the other side, where Shadow waited. He shook the dirt from his fur.

Taylor brushed the grime from her pant legs and jacket. "Good boy. You knew a way out we couldn't see."

"I'll be." Wyatt also wiped the remnants of the fallen tree from his clothes. "Shadow, you're one smart dog."

"That he is."

Wyatt squeezed her arm. "Thank you for trusting his gut."

"I almost didn't, but something told me to. I couldn't make the same mistake twice." Taylor examined the area. "Which way now?"

"There's a path to your right that leads toward the park station. We're almost home free." Wyatt skirted around more fallen trees.

Twenty minutes later, Taylor sped out of the empty park station's parking lot. "The others must have made it out safely. I'll check." She hit her sergeant's number on the Bluetooth and waited.

"Taylor. You safe?"

"Yes, sir. Had a close call, but Shadow led us out of a dangerous situation. Did you see any of the hunters shooting at us?"

"Nothing," her sergeant said. "I don't understand how they keep evading us. Wyatt, are you sure there aren't any hidden paths in the park?"

"None that I'm aware of. We need that map Fred mentioned."

"I'll contact him to find—"

Another call beeped on the line.

"Sir, I have another call coming in. Chat later." She didn't wait for his response, but took the second call. "Grant here."

Clapping sounded over the airwaves.

Taylor gripped the steering wheel tighter. "Who's there?"

"Just giving you a standing ovation for escaping the maze my hunters tried to trap you in. Nicely done." The robotic voice filtered through the Bluetooth.

Shadow barked.

"You, too, Shadow."

Taylor shifted her gaze to Wyatt's.

His contorted face told her he thought of the same thing.

How had this person known Shadow's name?

"This is Ridge, I presume." Taylor swerved onto the side of the road and stopped.

"Smart girl."

Taylor plucked her cell phone from its holder and quickly texted her leader, asking him to trace the current call on her police-issued phone. "How do you keep finding us?" Taylor caught her leader's reply and instruction to keep the caller talking.

"That's for me to know and you not to find out." He snickered. "Wyatt, how's Levi doing?"

Wyatt jerked straighter in his seat. "You stay away from my son."

"Tsk. Tsk. Simmer down, Cowboy. You interfered four years ago and your wife paid the price. Will your son pay the price this time?"

"What are you talking about?" Wyatt's tone turned into a growl.

"Don't you know? Your wife's accident wasn't an accident. I caused it."

Wyatt and Taylor both sucked in a breath.

"And now you'll lose your son for your interference. Time's up. Nice try tracing my call." *Click.*

Wyatt banged on the console. "Go, Taylor! Get back to the ranch."

Taylor gunned the gas, her tires spinning on the loose gravel as she veered her cruiser back onto the highway.

They had to save Levi from the evil Ridge.

No way would Taylor let him take Levi from Wyatt, too.

Wyatt jumped from Taylor's cruiser and whipped out his Glock, darting toward his ranch's front entrance as blood swooshed in his eardrums. He didn't know how much more heartache he could take. *Why, God? Why?* Why would a God of love allow such evil? Evil that killed his wife and threatened his son. He fished his keys out of his left pocket, but his shaky fingers lost hold and they thudded onto the veranda.

Taylor took the steps two at a time and scooped up the keys. "Let me help." She unlocked the front door and pushed it open.

Get it together. Wyatt silently chastised himself and flew into his home. "Dad! Where are you?"

Frank Hoyt appeared in the foyer, coffee cup in hand. His gaze shifted to Wyatt's gun. "Son, what's got you all worked up?"

"Is Levi okay?" Wyatt hated the terror lacing his question, but right now, his full panic mode had taken over every thought, and he struggled to contain all the what-ifs running through his mind.

His father's eyes widened. "He's sleeping. All is quiet. Why?"

Taylor stepped beside Wyatt and placed her hand on his gun, lowering his arm. "Wyatt, no one followed us home."

Wyatt stowed his gun. "I want to see my son."

His father gripped Wyatt's shoulders. "First, calm down and tell me what's going on."

Taylor wiggled out of her coat. "Our suspect just called us on my police-issued cell phone, claiming responsibility for Lisa's death."

Frank Hoyt let out a sharp cry. "What?"

"Yes, Dad. He caused Lisa's 'accident.'" Wyatt air-quoted *accident*. "Says it was for my interference four years ago."

His father brought Wyatt into a bear hug. "It's gonna be okay. God is in control."

Wyatt jerked out of his hold. "Is He? It doesn't appear that way. Not from where I'm standing." He hustled down the hallway and up the stairs, regretting his two-year-old temper tantrum. But he couldn't help it. His son was his life.

Without his son, he had nothing.

He paused at Levi's door, taking deep cleansing breaths. He would not enter his son's room in his present state. Wyatt eased open the door, peeking at his son. The night-light in the corner illuminated Levi sleeping, hugging his favorite stuffed animal.

Thank You, God. Ugh! How could he question God in one breath and thank Him in the next? His mother would be so disappointed in him. Another failure to add to his growing list.

He tiptoed into the room and lowered gently beside Levi. As much as he wanted to wake his son, he wouldn't. Wyatt drew the superhero comforter closer to Levi's neck, then softly kissed his forehead. "Love you, bud," he whispered.

Wyatt returned to the living room, where Taylor and Shadow sat nestled by the fireplace, explaining to his dad what had happened.

Frank pounded the armrest. "This Ridge person has to be stopped."

Wyatt plunked into the chair beside his father and took his hand in his. "He will, Dad. I'm sorry for my outburst earlier. I just couldn't fathom the thought of losing Levi. How did you cope after Kyle's death?"

"Not well, I'm sad to say."

Taylor stood. "I'll leave you gentlemen alone. Shadow, come." She walked in front of Wyatt's chair.

He clasped her hand. "No, stay, please. It's okay." Wyatt didn't want her to leave. Her presence brought him comfort. He suppressed a sigh. *You've fallen again, haven't you?* But he couldn't help it. He wanted Taylor Grant back in his life, but would she have him?

Taylor's gaze flipped to Frank's. "Is that okay?"

He smiled. "My son trusts you, so I trust you."

She sat on the couch, and Shadow hopped up beside her, snuggling close.

Wyatt's father stood and opened the fireplace doors. "You remember how I changed after Kyle's death, Wyatt? I did not handle it how I should have. I was a terrible father." He lifted the poker, stabbing at the coals. "I couldn't bear the thought of losing another child, so I did the best thing I could think of—treated all of you with a tyrannical fist. I figured that way, you'd never do what Kyle did. I failed him."

He turned and drilled his piercing gaze at Wyatt. "I couldn't stop the bullying, so I threatened the school. Even showed up at one of the parents' homes and punched the father. I'm surprised he didn't press charges."

"I had no idea, Dad." Wyatt leaned forward, resting his elbow on his knees. "I understand now that I have my own son. It was your way of grieving."

"Yes, but the sad part was it changed me. It took Jayla and Hazel's harshness toward me to make me see what I'd turned into. Your sisters were right, and it's something I'm ashamed of." Tears glistened in his father's eyes.

Wyatt sprang to his feet and hugged him. "That's not you anymore, Dad." A question burned deep within Wyatt. A question he had longed to ask for all these years, but never had the courage. He didn't want to know, but it was time. "Dad, did you blame me for Kyle's death?"

Frank Hoyt cried out before wrenching free of their embrace. "No! Wyatt, even if you had made it home before Kyle, he would have tried again. This was never your fault."

Tears pricked at the back of Wyatt's eyes. "I always thought you blamed me."

"I'm sorry," he whispered. "I only blamed myself because I couldn't stop my son's pain. That tore me apart."

Once again, Wyatt brought his father into a hug.

Shadow leaped off the couch and headbutted the two men.

Wyatt chuckled and turned to Taylor, raising his brow.

"He senses your distress and wants to give you love." She stood. "Can I join him?"

"Of course." Wyatt held his right arm out to her.

She walked into the hug. "You are both so special. I wish I had a father who cared so much."

Wyatt's breath hitched at her comment. He hated that her father had walked out on them. He didn't know what he'd do without Frank Hoyt's love and guidance.

Taylor retreated from their hold. "It's late. I'm heading to bed. See you in the morning. Shadow, come." The two trotted up the stairs and out of view.

"I'm turning in, too. Oh, Levi and I fed Ember."

"Thanks, Dad. I appreciate you coming."

His father squeezed Wyatt's shoulder, dipping his head in the direction Taylor had gone. "Son, don't let that one get away. Night." His father walked through the adjoining guest room's door.

His words lingered in Wyatt's mind. *Don't let that one get away.* But how could he convince Taylor Grant that they belonged together when she had broken his heart? He had to try.

Wyatt dashed up the stairs and lightly tapped on her door, mustering courage.

She eased it open. "Everything okay?"

Tell her. Tell her not to go away. Tell her how you feel.

He swallowed the emotions clogging his throat. "I—I just wanted to say thank you for today." *Chicken.*

"Anytime. Get some rest, okay? Night." She closed the door. *Ugh!*

His shoulders slouched as he trudged down the hall to his bedroom. It was for the best.

At least that was what his head said.

His heart didn't agree.

FOURTEEN

Buzzing jerked Wyatt from dreams that rotated between kissing Taylor and a frantic chase through a maze of shoulder-height prickly thorn bushes, a masked madman hot on his trail. He reached over and banged his alarm clock to stop the annoying sound, but realized it had been his cell phone. He cracked open an eye to catch the time. Five o'clock in the morning. Who's calling so early? Wyatt snatched the phone and checked his messages.

The caller snickered. "Rise and shine," the robotic voice said.

Wyatt lurched upright in his bed, alert.

"I hope you had a good sleep, because I know you're at a nearby ranch and there are only so many in this region. Process of elimination. I *will* find you. Don't think you and Levi are safe." More laughing sailed through the speaker before the line went dead.

Wyatt tossed his phone back on the nightstand. He whipped off his buffalo plaid comforter and placed his bare feet on the cool hardwood floor, sending chills up his legs. But he didn't mind. It helped jolt him fully awake. He rose and meandered to the window, parting the blinds.

Darkness hung over his property. The barn's light revealed a dense blanket of fog hovering like an eerie presence threatening to consume his ranch in one gigantic bite. A shudder snaked up his spine and settled in his neck muscles, locking them tight. Why did he get the feeling they were being watched? The caller had said he'd find them, meaning he hadn't yet.

Or had he, and he was simply taunting Wyatt? Waiting. Watching.

He scanned the backyard, but nothing materialized.

His cursory inspection didn't satisfy Wyatt, so he hastily dressed in jeans and a green plaid flannel shirt. He wouldn't be able to get back to sleep anyway, so why not check the grounds to be safe? Wyatt also dreaded more dreams of kissing the woman he could never have.

His cell phone buzzed, and he stiffened. Not again.

Wyatt snatched the device from the nightstand and read the screen. Iris. He hit Answer. "You're calling early, sis. What's up?"

"Can't I call and check in on my brother?"

"Dad texted you, didn't he?"

She guffawed. "Good guess. He was worried about you. I wasn't expecting to get you live, though. I wanted to leave you a message to let you know I'm thinking about you today and praying."

Wyatt clamped his eyes shut and plopped back onto the bed. "Thank you."

"He also told me that a beautiful woman and her dog are staying at your ranch. Spill, Wyatt. Who is she? Inquiring minds want to know."

He scratched the back of his head. "You mean my sisters? Let me guess. You sent a group text to them."

She snickered. "I couldn't resist. Dish, brother."

He had never told his family about Taylor. In fact, yesterday was the first time anyone had met her, but Wyatt had only shared minimal details with his father when he arrived. He had to explain her presence. "Nothing to tell. We dated two years ago, but she ended it suddenly and moved."

"But now she's back? Dad said she and her dog are protecting you and Levi."

"Yes, she recently returned to the area. This suspect also targeted her, so we're hiding out here. Oh, I lent her some of your clothes. Sorry."

"No prob. You care for her, don't you? I can hear it in your voice."

How could he answer Iris's question? Of all his sisters, Wyatt was the closest to her. She'd see right through him anyway. "I do, but, Iris, she already broke my heart once."

"It's been four years since Lisa passed. You deserve someone special."

"I can't open up again, especially with Levi's heart on the line, too."

"Let God lead you. He'll show you."

Wyatt flinched at her statement. "Will He? He's allowed too much heartache in my life. I'm assuming Dad told you what's going on?"

"Yes. I know you've been through a lot and now Levi is in danger, but God is there."

"Why can't I feel him?"

"Are you looking in the right places, Wyatt? God is everywhere. Remember that even though you can't feel Him, He's there. That's what faith is all about—trust. Clouds may cover the sky, but the sun is still there, shining brightly. It's the same with God. He's there in our storms."

Wyatt approached his nightstand and opened the drawer. Lisa's Bible still lay where she left it four years ago. He fingered the cracked leather binding, stopping at her name engraved beside a cross. "You sound like Mom. How did you get so wise?"

"Believe me, I falter, too, bro. But when I'm dropping into a fiery wilderness, I have to trust that my parachute will hold me." She paused. "Wyatt, trust that God will hold you, too."

"Thank you for the pep talk. I'll give it some thought." He closed the drawer. "Right now, I need to ensure my property is safe."

"Okay. Say hi to Dad for me. Love you."

"You, too, sis." He ended the call and pocketed his phone before heading out of his room. He hesitated in front of Levi's door, listening for movement.

Silence.

Good, his son was still sleeping.

Wyatt continued down to the lower level, stopping inside the kitchen.

Taylor sat at the island, nursing a cup of coffee. "Hey there. You're up early."

He hit the espresso machine's button, and the grinder pulverized the beans, its deafening roar filling the room. "You, too. Couldn't sleep?"

"'Fraid not. I keep going over in my mind who's leaking information."

"Come up with anything?"

"Zilch. Why are you up?"

"I got a disturbing message from Ridge." He brought out his phone and played the recording.

Taylor sat straighter on the island stool. "We have to check your property."

"That's exactly what I intend to do. Just needed some quick fuel first." His coffee finished dispensing, and he lifted it from the tray, sipping.

Taylor scrunched up her nose. "How can you drink it black?"

"Only way. I love savoring the fresh bean taste. Cream weakens that." He walked to the fridge and removed a couple of yogurt cups. "Something to give us energy. Prebreakfast." He slid one across the island to her and withdrew a spoon, tapping it on her nose. "Anyone tell you you're cute when you crinkle your nose?"

She froze.

Oh man. He hadn't meant to share that thought out loud.

He was listening to Iris too much. "Sorry. Just an observation." *Change the subject.* "Eat up and we'll head out to the barn. I'd like to take Ember for a ride to check the property. I'll make sure Dad is aware so he can watch Levi. Sound good?"

"Sure." She plunged her spoon into her opened yogurt.

Fifteen minutes later, Wyatt placed a saddle on Ember and

led her out of the barn to Taylor, waiting by the door. Shadow sat at her feet.

A question rose.

How would he ever be able to ride with her arms around his back? *Set it aside, dude. Concentrate on the task at hand.*

Secure his domain from potential threats.

"I only have one horse, so we'll ride together." He mounted Ember and patted the saddle's seat. "Your turn." He removed his foot and held out his hand.

"I got it." She placed her foot into the stirrup and launched herself up and over, tucking her arms around his waist.

"Impressive. How many times have you been on a horse?"

"Counting the other day with you? Once." She giggled like a schoolgirl. "I guess I learn quickly from the best cowboy."

He glanced over his shoulder and dipped his cowboy hat. "Aw shucks, ma'am."

"How big is your property?"

Taylor had been to the ranch twice when they dated, but only to the homestead.

"It's smaller than most. Eight hundred acres. I only have two part-time ranch hands. They come in and take care of the property every few days." He squeezed his legs into Ember's sides. "Let's go, girl."

Ember trotted forward.

"Shadow, come!" Taylor yelled.

The dog ran beside Ember, keeping pace. The group traveled past the ranch, barn and shed housing Wyatt's property, and headed west toward the tree line.

The sun began its ascent over the mountain, edging its golden head above the peaks. Daybreak was Wyatt's favorite time of the day. Peaceful. Serene. Still. What more could one ask for?

Even though he questioned God, he couldn't deny the Creator's handiwork.

And right now—with the beautiful woman at his back—he wanted to get lost in the moment.

And never let go.

Suddenly, Shadow emitted a guttural growl, invading Wyatt's thoughts of serenity.

The dog zoomed toward the property's edge, which stretched parallel to a secondary highway.

Taylor tightened her grip around Wyatt's waist.

Wyatt's heartbeat skyrocketed as a question tumbled through his mind.

Had Ridge found them, after all?

Taylor released her tight grip around Wyatt's waist and patted him on the shoulder, pointing to the fence dividing a section of his land from the road. "Follow Shadow. He's alerting to something."

The sun's rays filtered through the hovering fog, casting shadows across the property, and chills prickled Taylor's body. She placed her hand on her sidearm, grateful that Sergeant Mitchell had granted her request to keep her gun and radio while staying at Wyatt's ranch. They required extra protection and Taylor had argued that she wouldn't let Ridge take Levi again.

Shadow barked and slipped through a narrow opening in the wooden fence, hurtling onto the highway.

Wyatt guided Ember toward a locked metal gate and stopped by a keypad. He leaned over and punched in a code. The gate opened and Wyatt kicked the horse's flank, clucking her onward.

Taylor held on to Wyatt's waist tighter as the gate automatically closed behind them. She wasn't scared of horseback riding, but the last time she rode on Ember, the horse had bucked, and Taylor wouldn't take any risks of falling off.

They caught up to Shadow, who now sat beside a portion of the fence in the road's curve, barking.

Wyatt tugged on Ember's reins. "Whoa, girl." The horse stopped.

"What is it, Shadow?" Taylor dismounted and approached her K-9. She unclipped her Maglite from her duty belt and turned it on, shining it around the region.

But nothing materialized in the light's beam.

"What is Shadow alerting to?" Wyatt climbed off Ember and held her reins.

"No idea. There's nothing here."

"Could it have been an animal? Another red fox?" Wyatt guided Ember to the fence and tethered her.

Taylor shone her light, scouring the road, field and tree line. "Possibly, but whatever caused Shadow to take off is gone." She unhooked her radio. "I'm going to check to see if there's a cruiser in the area."

"Good idea. That would make me feel better. I get the sense that Shadow wouldn't typically bolt after an animal."

"He doesn't. I trained him that way, but something sure spooked him." Taylor unhooked her radio and identified herself to Dispatch before asking if there was a cruiser in their location. She scanned the area again as Dispatch checked. Clouds had drifted in, hampering the sunrise. Meteorologists had predicted a cluster of fierce storms would blanket their region over the next few days. Just what they needed—more thunderstorms among threats from a criminal mastermind.

Taylor tapped her foot, waiting for Dispatch. *Come on.*

Her radio squawked a reply. "Grant, a cruiser patrolled that region thirty minutes ago."

"Did they report any suspicious activity?"

"Negative. Do you require assistance?"

Did they? She couldn't really redirect a cruiser here on a whim that Shadow sensed something. She must have more concrete evidence of foul play or danger.

"No. Will keep you posted if I do."

"Copy that."

Taylor reattached her radio on her belt. "I'm sure the constable on duty would have reported anything out of the ordinary." She eyed Shadow. "Boy, what did you alert to?"

The dog's ears perked up. *Woof!*

Taylor sighed. "This is out of the norm for him. I don't like it."

Wyatt pointed to the sky. "And I'm not crazy about those ominous clouds. Levi doesn't need more storms."

"I know. The weather report says the storms will persist for the rest of the week." Taylor observed how the cloud had now covered 80 percent of the rising sun, leaving one ray of light filtering through the fog. She pointed. "Look at that. Such beauty."

Wyatt peered upward, then back to her, his expression coiling into disgust. "Seriously? The clouds are overtaking the sun and I'm sure they're filled with lots of hail, rain and wind. How is that beautiful?"

Taylor placed her hands on her hips. "Where you see threatening storms and danger, I see God's beauty." She pointed to the horizon. "Look at how the sun peeks through the clouds, displaying a ray of light into the fog. Breathtaking."

Wyatt grunted. "I wish I could see the positive like you do. I used to, but lately, I've been finding it hard."

She inched closer to his side and grazed his arm, letting her fingers linger. "I get it. You and your family have had their share of tribulations, but there comes a time in life when we have to trust God and let the storms transform us instead of turning us into someone bitter." She bit her lip. "Like my mother. Please, don't be like her."

His expression softened, and he squeezed her hand, rubbing it with his thumb. "You're right. Maybe I need someone positive in my life, like you, to guide me in that direction. You're a good friend."

Good friend? What if she wanted more? *God, what are You doing to me? You know why I can't commit.*

Taylor drew her hand away from his and stepped backward. "I'm sure Iris will help keep you grounded."

She didn't miss the flinch distorting his handsome face.

You did it again, Taylor. Stop breaking his heart.

The problem was…she also was doing the same to her own.

Shadow growled and cemented his stance in front of them, his gaze directed at the tree line.

Taylor straightened and shone her light.

Eyes glistened in the beam seconds before an arrow and flash of white flew.

"Get down!" She hauled her Glock from her holster and fired.

The arrow hit the fence, barely missing them.

The assailant ducked back into the forest.

Taylor grabbed her radio and requested backup to their location, giving them details of the archer in the woods. "I need to follow and catch this suspect."

"Wait." Wyatt pointed at something white on the fence. "What is that?"

The dawn setting hid what lay in the shadows.

Taylor gasped.

The arrow pierced a target practice sheet and lodged into the wooden fence. A perfect bull's-eye. A crude message was written under the arrow.

Found you.

"No! Let your constables comb through the woods. We have to get back to the ranch." Wyatt untethered Ember and got on, extending his hand. "Quick, we have to go!"

Taylor stowed her weapon and mounted the horse.

Wyatt spun Ember in a tight one-eighty and nudged her ribs, clucking his tongue. "Hyah! Let's go, girl!"

The horse bolted forward.

"Shadow, protect!" Taylor commanded her dog, pointing in the direction of Wyatt's home. She looked over her shoulder and spotted her K-9 obeying her directive, but her breath hitched as headlights knifed through the fog from behind, bearing down on them.

And approaching at a hair-raising speed, their intent obvious. Drive them off the road.

She whipped out her weapon. "Go! Go! Someone's coming."

Shadow barreled back through the fence line onto Wyatt's property.

The engine's roar grew louder, the danger closing in.

And threatening the lives of all those hiding at the ranch.

FIFTEEN

Wyatt's stomach twisted into an impenetrable knot, turning his fear into terror as questions tumbled through his mind. How had Ridge found them? Had he already breached Wyatt's ranch and hurt Levi—and his father? *No, God, no! Please keep them safe. Do what You will with me, save my family.* Wyatt squeezed his legs into Ember, intensifying his command for her to gallop faster. "Go, Ember!"

The sorrel horse increased her speed, but the headlights crept closer from the rear, and Wyatt refused to look over his shoulder. He had to concentrate on keeping them safe. After all, the woman at his back meant the world to him.

Even if she didn't feel the same.

Wyatt steered Ember toward the gate, pulled on the reins to slow her long enough for Wyatt to punch in the code. The automated gate opened and they trotted through.

A bullet pinged off the metal railing, sending Wyatt's pulse hammering.

Taylor returned fire, shooting three rounds at the vehicle before resecuring her hold around Wyatt's waist.

The gate shut behind them, and Wyatt flicked Ember's reins. The horse increased her speed, racing toward the homestead.

Wyatt caught a glimpse of Shadow in his peripheral vision, pelting across the yard. The dog was running at an amazing speed. He leaped over a cluster of bushes and dodged into the backyard.

Sirens sounded in the distance. Additional help was on the way. Good. Wyatt had to get to the house. Daylight had ascended, and he glanced right for a clearer look at their perpetrators. The white pickup chasing them had tinted windows, hiding the driver. Something niggled at the back of Wyatt's brain. Wait! He'd seen that truck before. But where?

Flashing lights appeared in the opposite direction, gaining ground toward them.

The truck did a quick U-turn and sped back down the road.

Taylor slapped his back. "Bushes, Wyatt." She pointed.

Pay attention, man. He had been too deep in thought. "Hang on!" Wyatt kicked Ember's flank to speed her up. If he tried to stop his horse, she'd probably send Taylor flying again.

The horse raced and leaped over the bushes, landing in perfect formation, like he'd taught her. *Good girl.* Wyatt diverted Ember to the left and brought her to a stop in front of the ranch's veranda.

Taylor dismounted, bent over and drew in several quick breaths.

"You okay?" Wyatt climbed off and tied the reins to the railing.

Taylor's eyes narrowed as she marched into his personal space and slapped his chest. "Never do that again." She pivoted, bounded up the steps and ran inside, letting the screen door slam behind her.

If the situation wasn't so serious, Wyatt would have laughed at her reaction, but he refrained and rubbed Ember. "Good girl. I'll be back." He scanned the front yard for any suspicious movement, but nothing skulked in the bushes they had just jumped over, or in the trees on the edge of the property. All was quiet again.

But their location was now compromised.

Wyatt gritted his teeth and entered his home. He wiped his cowboy boots on the mat before taking the stairs two at a time. He had to check on his son.

Wyatt eased open Levi's door and stuck his head inside.

The race car bed was empty, sheets rumpled. "Levi! Where are you?" Wyatt checked the bathroom. Empty. He hurried down the stairs and met Taylor as she let Shadow in the rear door. "Have you seen Dad or Levi?"

"No, I was concentrating on Shadow."

Laughter filtered through the living room.

Wyatt spun around and charged toward the guest room, yanking the door open. "Levi!"

His son was bouncing on the bed while his grandfather attempted to tickle him. The duo stopped and stared at Wyatt as if nothing in the world was wrong.

"Levi, stop jumping on the bed. How many times do I have to tell you that? You know better!" Wyatt failed to subdue the frustration in his tone. Frustration from fear of losing his son, not really from his son's actions.

Levi dropped onto the bed, his lip quivering.

"Wyatt, what's going on?" Frank Hoyt hugged his grandson. "You're scaring him."

Wyatt puffed out an elongated breath and approached. "Levi, I'm sorry. Daddy was just worried."

Taylor scooted around Wyatt and held out her hand. "Levi, how about you help me feed Shadow? He needs his Wheaties."

Tears glistened in Levi's eyes, his lips curving upward. "Can I, Papa?"

"Of course." Wyatt turned to face Taylor and mouthed, *Thank you.*

She dipped her head in acknowledgment.

"Miss Taylor, do you really feed Shadow cereal?" Levi's innocent question blared in the room as he latched on to Taylor's extended hand. The pair proceeded toward the door.

"Sometimes." She turned and winked at Wyatt.

His heart flickered and sent warmth flushing through his body.

The duo skipped out of the room.

"She's great with Levi," his father said, drawing Wyatt's attention away from the woman. "He talks about her nonstop."

"She is." Wyatt plopped onto the bed, resting his elbows on his knees. "Just hate that when this is all over, Levi's little heart will be broken when she leaves."

His father placed his hand on Wyatt's back. "What about *your* heart?"

"I'm afraid it's already broken. She only wants to be a friend, Dad."

"And you want more?"

"She's the only woman I've been interested in since Lisa passed." He shifted his position and faced his father. "Why would God let me fall for someone who wasn't interested?"

"You're asking the wrong Hoyt about God." His father stood and walked to his suitcase, drawing out a plaid shirt. "Your mother would have the right words to say, but all I can give you is one. Trust."

"I'm trying, but He's not helping, and to add salt to the wound, our hiding spot here at the ranch is compromised." Wyatt explained what happened. "I raced home to make sure Levi was safe, and he wasn't in his room. I panicked and took it out on him." He hung his head. "What kind of father am I?"

His dad took two strides to bridge the gap between them and placed his hands on Wyatt's shoulders. "Son, never say that. Levi's life was at stake. You were worried. No one could ever fault you for losing your temper. Just explain that to him. Don't do what I did and bury it deep inside."

The front doorbell rang.

Wyatt stood. "I'm guessing that's the constables Dispatch sent." He hugged his father. "Thank you for being here."

"Anytime. You know that."

Wyatt exited the guest room and headed to the front door, rolling his shoulders as he directed courage into his tense muscles. He had to consult with the constables on a plan to keep his son safe.

Wyatt would not let Ridge drive him and Levi from their home.

"Sir, you didn't need to come." Taylor handed Sergeant Bryan Mitchell a coffee. "Wyatt, Levi and I are fine. Constable Elliott and I could have handled this." Taylor loved that he cared so much, but she hated to be a nuisance. Clearly, from his contorted expression, he had been worried when her call came in for backup at their location.

He took the mug and leaned closer. "I had to check on my girl. You okay?"

The tone in his voice replaced her previous anxiety over the incident with a soothing calmness that settled throughout her body. *Why couldn't you have been my father?* Losing Ken Grant had left a gaping hole in Taylor's life. One that no one else had ever filled. Until Bryan came along. "I'm a little shaken, but I'll be fine."

Wyatt and Elliott had left to do a sweep of the property to ensure the suspects had indeed left the vicinity. Frank was entertaining Levi and Shadow in the family room. Wyatt had said he didn't want his son hearing any of their conversation, so he gave Levi a quick breakfast and tasked his father to take over.

"Do you think Wyatt will leave the ranch and go to an undisclosed location?"

"Doubtful. He was pretty adamant when I suggested it." She poured cream in her coffee and stirred. "I don't blame him. Levi has been uprooted enough with all that's happened."

Wyatt and Constable Elliott shuffled into the room.

Taylor removed two mugs from the cupboard and poured in the dark roasted coffee, passing them each one. "Did you find anything suspicious?"

"Nothing. Whoever had tried to run us off the road is gone."

Wyatt sipped his coffee. "I wish I'd gotten the plates of that truck. I know I've seen it before."

"I'm sure there are a few white pickups in Kesbush Bay so don't beat yourself up. I should have gotten the plate number, too." Taylor passed Elliott the cream and sugar. "It all happened so fast."

"CSU is on their way to get pics of the arrow and practice sheet," Elliott said. "Thanks for the coffee. It hits the spot. Cooler out this morning."

"And a storm is brewing," Bryan added. "Can we chat in your dining room, Wyatt?"

"Of course. This way." Wyatt extended his arm to direct them. The group sat.

Bryan cleared his throat. "First, I'm glad you're all safe. That was a close call." His gaze shifted to Wyatt. "Any idea how this Ridge found your ranch? It's well hidden. I barely found it myself."

"Perhaps someone leaked where I live." Wyatt cupped his hands around his mug. "Or, he somehow found out I was on a ranch and there are only a few in the area. Process of elimination. I sensed earlier that someone was watching." He raised his brow. "But we never disclosed we were on a ranch, so how did he know?"

Elliott fumbled with his mug, spilling coffee on the table. "Oh no. That might be my fault. I might have let the word *ranch* slip, but only when we were out searching with the others. I'm sorry." He hung his head. "After Constable Day's death, I've had a hard time focusing."

Taylor leaned closer to Elliott. "Her death hit us hard. It's understandable."

"She's right, Elliott. We're not sure that's how Ridge found out. I still feel there's a mole at the station." Bryan slapped his hand on the table. "I haven't been able to plug the leak."

"Has Dr. Oke shared anything about Sam's autopsy?" Taylor grabbed a nearby napkin and wiped up Elliott's spilled coffee.

Bryan's eyes brightened. He fished out a notebook from his pocket, flipped it open. "Yes. She called late yesterday. I'm still waiting on the full report, but her fall was the fatal injury. However, her body had multiple contusions and knife wounds. Her right eye was swollen shut, likely from blunt-force impact. Her neck had distinct ligature marks, consistent with strangulation."

Taylor's jaw dropped. "We were right. She was beaten before someone pushed her, but they also tried to strangle her?"

"And stab her. We know the cell phone Levi found was stolen. My guess is someone tried to determine if she or anyone else saw what was on it." Bryan's eyes narrowed. "I want this person behind bars. They must pay for what they did to one of our own."

"And we will find Ridge. Sam deserves justice, but right now we need a plan to keep Wyatt and Levi safe." Taylor hated to shift the conversation, but they were the priority.

"And I'm not moving my son, Sergeant Mitchell. He doesn't do well with displacement."

Bryan raised his hands. "I get it, Wyatt. I'm low on resources with Sam's death, but I'll place a cruiser outside your property line 24/7. That work?"

"Yes, sir." Wyatt's gaze shifted to Taylor. "You're good to leave Taylor and Shadow on the premises, too, right? With her weapon?"

He addressed Taylor. "What if we get a call requiring Shadow's keen nose?"

"Call the Labrador City detachment. They have a top-notch K-9 unit. I'm not leaving Levi and Wyatt's side, sir." She braced herself for an argument.

Bryan grunted. "I know not to argue with you." He finished his coffee and stood. "Okay, time to roll, Elliott. You take the first shift here at the ranch. I cordoned off the road and fence where the arrow is lodged. You guide CSU when they arrive."

Elliott pushed himself up. "Copy. Heading there now. Be careful, Taylor, and call if you see any suspicious movement on the property."

Taylor rose out of the chair. "I will. Be safe. Remember, heads on a swivel."

He waggled his finger at her. "You keep stealing my expression." Elliott chuckled and left.

Bryan put on his jacket and brought Taylor into an embrace. "Please don't take any risks. I need you to stay safe."

Tears prickled at the back of her eyes, his compassion warming her heart. "Copy that. Keep me posted on any developments."

He pulled away and turned to Wyatt. "I'm also counting on you. Watch her back."

"I will, sir." Wyatt led the group to the front door. "My dad is a park warden, so he's also trained in law enforcement."

"Good, I need lots of protection for my girl. She's the daughter we never had." His voice quivered.

Taylor reached around him and opened the door. "Love you, sir. Now go before you make me cry."

He chuckled and scurried down the veranda steps.

"He's a great guy." Wyatt closed the door, locking it. "I'm glad you have him in your life."

"Me, too." Taylor watched through the door's side glass panel, as her leader—and father figure—disappeared down the laneway. She wiped the escaped tear from her cheek.

Her cell phone dinged, announcing a text. She removed it from her pocket and swiped the screen. "Good. Fred found the map and sent a picture."

"Best news I've heard today."

"I'll grab my laptop and we can take a better look. Maybe you'll recognize the terrain." Taylor pumped her fist in the air.

Finally, a win.

Taylor's phone rang, interrupting her celebration. She checked the screen and grimaced. "It's my mom. I should take this."

"I'll meet you in the dining room." Wyatt sauntered down the hallway.

Taylor hit Answer. "What's up, Mom?"

"Is that any way to start a conversation with your mother?" She laced her question with sarcasm.

Taylor cringed. "Sorry, Mom. It's been a rough few days."

"Since you accused me of keeping secrets about your father, I have more news you'll want to hear."

Taylor plunked onto the deacon's bench in the hallway. Something told her she'd need to sit for this conversation. "What?"

"He passed away last night, Taylor." Her mother's voice quivered. The man had walked out on them, but even after all these years of heartache, Terri Grant still loved him.

Taylor clamped her eyes shut, waiting for remorse of the loss to set in. However, her father had never once reached out to her after he'd walked out the door. Not on her birthday. Not at Christmas.

"You still there, Taylor?"

She sighed. "I am. Sorry for your loss."

"That's it? He was your father."

Taylor opened her eyes and hopped to her feet. "My father? He ceased being my father when he walked out of my life, Mom." *Ugh! Now who's the bitter one?*

"Look, I realize the lack of his presence in your life is tough, but doesn't God command us to forgive?"

Her mother was talking about God? Taylor couldn't remember the last time she did. "Wait, I didn't think you believed any longer?"

"I've been going to church again. God is teaching me about forgiveness and I've rededicated my life to Him."

Good for you, Mom. Could this be what it takes to mend their relationship? She wanted her mother back in her life. "I'm glad, Mom. And you're right, God commands us to forgive. I have to process this first."

"I understand. Can we meet for coffee sometime? I want back into your life."

Hope surged through Taylor, relaxing her tense muscles. "I'd like that, Mom. I'm working a case right now, but will call you after it's wrapped up."

"Sounds good. I'll be praying for you."

"I could use them, thanks." Taylor paused. "I'm glad you called. Talk later."

"Love you." Her mother hung up before Taylor could respond.

I do love you, too, Mom.

Taylor stuffed her phone into her pocket and nearly skipped toward the dining room, a lightness in her step concerning her mother. Perhaps they had turned a corner in their relationship.

If only she and Wyatt could solve this case as well.

After spending the rest of the day with his son and father while Taylor consulted on various video calls, Wyatt brought two cups of hot chocolate to the dining room table where Taylor waited to go over additional information her sergeant had provided later in the day. They also wanted to do a deep dive of the map Fred had sent.

Lightning flashed, and seconds later, thunder exploded, shaking the house.

"That was a close one. Good thing Levi is cuddling with G'pa or we'd be hearing lots of screaming coming from a five-year-old." Wyatt hesitated, unsure of how to extend his sympathies regarding her father's death. "I'm sorry again about your father."

"Thank you."

She smiled, but it didn't reach her lips. Wyatt read the strain behind her expression. Her father's death took more out of her than she would admit.

Time to change the subject.

He passed her a mug topped with lots of marshmallows and

whipped cream. "Fuel for our investigation and dessert after the yummy supper you made."

"My pleasure. After all, I'm invading your home. It's the least I could do. Plus, homemade mac and cheese is my fave." She took the cup and sipped, leaving a dollop of cream on the end of her nose. "So good."

"You have a little left." Wyatt smiled and tapped her nose to remove the white goodness. He stuck his finger in his mouth, concentrating on the task at hand. Anything to divert his attention from the beautiful woman in front of him. He loved when she wore her long, wavy dirty-blond hair down, but he resisted the urge to tuck a stray curl behind her ear. "Glad you like it. Shall we look at this map? I printed a copy, but it's pretty small."

Wyatt had to change the subject, or he'd get lost in the Taylor-can-you-stay-in-my-life pit. He smoothed the paper out and studied the hand-drawn map of the Kesbush Gorge area, including various trails, clusters of trees, cliffs, the labyrinth maze, cliff path, river and waterfalls.

She turned her laptop around, the map magnified on the screen. "Does any of this look familiar to you?"

"I feel like this is a treasure map and there should be an X to mark the spot leading to the hidden gold." Wyatt chuckled before tapping on a crude replication of a red bridge. "This is the gorge bridge that led to the other side of the canyon back in the day and where I spotted the suspects." He circled his index finger around different trails. "These are the paths that lead to various other campsites, picnic spots, fishing holes and..." He let his thought trail off as he inched closer. "Wait a minute. I'm not sure what this is."

"What?"

He pointed. "Here. Pete drew a tiny row of x's under the stick trees."

"What could it be referring to?"

"No idea. That's a densely wooded stretch of land. No rivers. Just forest." He ran his finger along the *x*-path. "It appears to extend throughout portions of the park and end at the mouth of where the Labrador Sea meets the North Atlantic Ocean."

"Huh." Taylor slouched, folding her arms over her chest, tapping her index finger on her forearm. "And there's nothing there that you can think of?"

"No." Levi's drawing entered his mind. "Did Sergeant Mitchell have any updates on the airport?"

"He has a team monitoring the runways. Constables have also interviewed employees, but nothing substantial to report. Few small planes coming and going, but that's normal."

"Okay, what else did your leader send you?"

Taylor set down her mug and clicked on her keyboard. "Digital forensics finally reported back on the video Denise took with her phone." She leaned closer as she read her screen. "Says here the audio is too distorted for a viable voice match. The visual isn't any better—too much motion blur to capture a clear frame of the suspect for facial recognition. Not surprised. Denise was obviously shaking when she took it. Understandably so. Poor thing."

"Another dead end." Wyatt slapped his palm on the table. "We need a break. What about the pictures she took?"

"Only side profiles and his face was covered, so nothing to help with facial recognition."

"Anything more on the interrogations of the two suspects they caught?"

She gave a small shake of her head, lips curving downward into a frown in obvious defeat.

Defeat Wyatt had a hard time shaking like the unending cluster of thunderstorms hovering over Kesbush Bay.

He stood and sauntered to the window overlooking the backyard. Hail hammered the property, pinging off the barn roof in the distance. "So, we still have no way of identifying Ridge, and right now, he could be watching somewhere close, planning his next attack." His shoulders drooped. "I hate to be negative, but I need this to be over."

Her hand rested on his back, and he jolted. He hadn't heard her stealthy approach. *You're losing it, Wyatt. Get. It. Together.*

He turned and faced her, examining her expression. Was now the right time to ask her? He had to know. "Taylor, why did you really break up with me? I thought we had something special going."

She staggered backward. "I just was at a point in my life where I didn't want to commit and when you talked about marriage and kids, I panicked."

Wyatt took one large step to get back into her personal space. This time, he didn't resist and tucked a stray hair behind her ear, leaning close. "And now? I'm pretty sure you're feeling what I'm feeling."

"I—I…can't." Her voice was barely audible.

Ugh! What wasn't she telling him? "Why did you really break up with me?" He moved closer. "I'm a big boy. I can take it."

She placed her hand on his chest and pushed, her eyes narrowing. "Stop asking me. I need a break from you right now. I'm going to bed to read. See you in the morning." She pivoted and marched out of the room, her footfalls fading into the background.

What just happened?

Wyatt huffed out a breath. *Why won't she tell me?*

God, why bring her back into my life only to have her break my heart again?

Taylor sank farther under the covers at two o'clock in the morning, her conversation with Wyatt on repeat like an annoying song of lament, echoing with heartache of what could have been but was beyond her reach. She pounded the bed. *Why, God? Why did You allow the cancer to take my hope of bearing a child?* Even though Taylor realized she could adopt, her heart's desire was to feel a child growing inside her womb—have the baby kick. She'd been robbed of that joy and the reality that it wouldn't happen left an ache she couldn't heal, especially when the doctor had explained her predicament after she woke from the surgery. They had hoped to extract the cancer without doing a full hysterectomy, but when they had a clear picture of what they were dealing with, her life trumped their decision. Not being able to have a child also stole her self-worth. Shame held her back from revealing the whole truth with Wyatt. She wanted nothing more than to tell him how she felt. Feelings that had morphed into what she now realized flowed through her body—love for Conservation Officer Wyatt Hoyt and his amazing son, Levi.

Taylor hated how she bolted from the dining room, but panic overwhelmed her. She did what she did best—fled when things got dicey. She'd been dealing with the news of her father's death, and when Wyatt probed into the past, it sent her over the edge. "Ugh!"

Shadow whimpered from his spot in the chair by the door. He lifted his head.

"Sorry, bud. I'm okay. Go to sleep."

Her dog lowered his head, resettling to rest. Good.

Coward. Just tell Wyatt.

Yes, that's what she'd do in the morning. It was time.

Time to confess her real reason for breaking his heart. Time to bare her true feelings.

God, I give that conversation to You. Give me Your words.

Taylor rolled over, her back facing the door and Shadow. *Help me sleep. I'm tired and I surrender to You.*

She sang her favorite hymn in her mind and slowly her body stilled, sleep luring her under.

A growl followed by a whimper jolted her awake. *Shadow?*

Puttering feet sounded and her muscles locked seconds before a pinprick stung her like a bee.

"Get her to the truck. Ridge will take out Wyatt. Ricky is grabbing Levi. Hurry!"

The abductor's raspy command registered only in Taylor's mind as her body succumbed to whatever drug entered her vein.

"Help!" Her feeble scream dissipated in the shadows, talons clawing into her flesh as hands lifted her and the darkness dragged her under with no hope of rescue or escape—just the crushing truth that she failed again to save those around her, including herself.

Crack! A roar of thunder jolted Wyatt awake. A faint rustle stirred from the lower level of his ranch—subtle, but enough to send goose bumps rippling across his arms. A hush fell over him as he waited to see if the sound was his overactive imagination. His alarm clock displayed two thirty in the morning.

Scrape, shuffle, scrape.

Wyatt sat up, his body alert.

This time, the sound intensified.

Someone was in the house.

Why wasn't Shadow barking? And why hadn't his house alarm alerted him?

Levi!

Wyatt sprang off his bed and snatched his phone from the nightstand. He grabbed a baseball bat from the closet before yanking his door open. He raised the bat and tiptoed down the hallway, a night-light guiding his way.

Crack!

The light snapped off, blanketing the ranch into total darkness.

A drumbeat echoed in Wyatt's head as he crept along the hall, feeling his way to Levi's room.

The door stood ajar—sending a chill coiling around Wyatt's spine.

Not good.

His heart rate spiked, his instincts shouted a warning, but he forced his hand to reach for the knob, fingers shaking as they encircled the cold metal.

A subtle movement sounded directly behind him—too close. A sudden prick stung his neck.

Spots flickered in his vision as his world faded and tilted.

His knees buckled as Taylor's scream bellowed nearby, but out of reach.

"We have your boy and girlfriend. You lose, Cowboy."

The assailant's words drifted into Wyatt's tunnel-like foggy mind in a muffled and jumbled woven mess, impossible to untangle.

He crumpled—helpless to grab anything to break his fall—and succumbed to the darkness.

SIXTEEN

Wyatt's head throbbed like a jackhammer, each pulse bringing a fresh flood of nausea. Darkness clung to him as he attempted to tunnel his way out of a black pit. Where was he? What happened? His thoughts weighed him down, his mind slow like molasses. *Wake up!* His body wasn't cooperating. Finally, coolness registered beneath him, along with the mixed scent of his son's dirty socks and crayons wafting nearby. Levi! Wyatt popped his eyes open. He was lying on the floor in front of Levi's room. His foggy brain lifted, bringing with it a recollection of the terrifying events. The sound behind him. The sting of a bee. Taylor's scream.

Then darkness.

He sat upright, regretting the quick movement as the room spun. Wyatt braced against the wall, dragging himself upward little by little. Hand over hand, he clawed his way to his feet, every movement sending stabbing pains into his throbbing head, his weak legs protesting. He parted his lips. *Dad, where are you? Shadow?* The questions in his head failed to come out of his mouth. *Get it together. Find your son and Taylor.*

He entered his boy's room. An empty bed. Levi's favorite stuffed animal lay on the floor. His suspicions confirmed. Someone had taken his son. Wyatt opened the nightstand drawer and removed Levi's superhero flashlight. He turned it on and stumbled to Taylor's room. Her door was open, her bed empty, revealing why she screamed. She was gone, too.

A whimper sounded behind Wyatt, and he pivoted.

A groggy Shadow tumbled from the chair and onto the floor.

"Shadow!" Wyatt hurried to the dog's side and squatted. "What's wrong, boy?"

The K-9 lifted his head and whined.

Wyatt rubbed the dog's fur, guessing that someone had drugged the shepherd. How long would it take before whatever the perp injected into the animal wore off? He'd have to test his mobility. Wyatt stood. "Shadow, come!" He laced the command with force.

With a low cry, Shadow pushed to his feet and swayed, but straightened on all fours.

Groggy, but coming around. Like Wyatt.

Wyatt had to check on his father. "Slow but steady, boy. Come."

Wyatt held tightly to the stair railing and limped down the steps. Shadow followed.

"Dad!" He shuffled to the guest room and edged open the door. What would he find?

"Dad, you awake?" Wyatt entered the room and flicked on the light. The power was back on. Had it been the storm that knocked it out or whoever invaded his ranch?

His father's body lay motionless on the bed.

"No!" Wyatt sprang forward and felt his dad's neck. A steady pulse throbbed under his fingertips. *Thank You, God*. He gently shook his father's shoulders. "Dad, wake up!"

Nothing.

He nudged him harder. "Dad?"

Shadow barked.

Good, the dog's senses were coming around, too. Obviously, the suspects hadn't given him a large dose. Just enough to knock them both out, but why?

Why not kill them?

His father moaned, interrupting Wyatt's silent questions.

"Dad, you okay?" Wyatt pulled back the comforter, assessing his father's condition.

Frank Hoyt rubbed his temples. "What happened? My head hurts."

"Dad, Levi and Taylor are gone." Panic pooled in his iced veins as a lump of fear lodged in his throat, constricting his airway. He drew in ragged, quick breaths.

His father eased into a seated position and squeezed Wyatt's shoulder. "Breathe, son. Inhale and exhale slowly."

Wyatt obeyed and took deep cleansing breaths, one at a time, until his elevated heart rate slowed. "What time is it?"

His father checked his watch. "Six."

Wyatt sprang from the bed. "Whatever they gave me had me under for almost four hours. We have to find Levi and Taylor."

"But how? What do you remember? I heard a crack and then someone hit me over the head."

"The crack was thunder. Then the hydro went out. I heard Taylor yell for help, then felt a pinprick. They drugged Shadow, too."

The dog nuzzled into Wyatt, whining.

Wyatt dropped to the floor and hugged the German shepherd. "We'll find her, boy. We have to."

"Did you call 911?"

"No, I just woke up and checked on Levi." Rising, he fished his cell phone from his pocket as the device buzzed. The screen displayed Unknown Caller.

Wyatt's muscles coiled, and he braced himself as he answered, putting the call on speaker. "Wyatt Hoyt."

"'Bout time you woke." The robotic voice blared in the room.

Shadow growled.

Wyatt's gaze shot to his father's, his entire body cementing. "Who is this? Ridge?"

"Good guess. Glad Shadow is coming along. Don't worry, he'll be fine. I don't hurt dogs."

Anger coiled in Wyatt's chest. "But you will hurt a child. You're sick."

"Simmer down."

Wyatt flinched. He'd heard that expression before. He rubbed his brow, trying to bring his fuzzy head into clear focus.

"And don't think Constable Elliott can help you. He's out cold and will be for hours. My men made sure of it."

Rage coiled around Wyatt's spine as fear knotted his gut. "What do you want for my son's return?"

"Simple. You."

Silence permeated the room, sending silent shivers of terror jabbing into Wyatt.

"Tell me how, and I'll be there."

His father scrambled off the bed and punched the mute button. "Son, you can't. That's exactly what he wants. You surrender and he still kills you, Levi and Taylor."

"Dad, I can't stay idle and do nothing. This is Levi we're talking about. My heart. Lisa's heart." How could his father say such a thing? He knew what it was like to lose a son.

"I've been in the clutches of a serial killer. My experience tells me he'll kill you all anyway." His father latched on to Wyatt's arm. "I'm not suggesting we do nothing. Time to call Taylor's sergeant. He'll know what to do."

"He—"

"Tick tock. Time's a-wastin'. What will it be?"

Wyatt understood what his father was saying, but Wyatt had to do something. Even if it cost him his life. He took the call off Mute. "I want assurance that Taylor and Levi are alive."

"Speak, boy."

"Papa? I'm scared. Can you come and get me?"

Wyatt released a breath of relief. "I will, Levi. You okay?"

"Yes, but—"

"Enough," Ridge replied. "I'm sorry to say, though, that your pretty girlfriend is still passed out. I guess I gave her too much of my special drug."

Wyatt's shoulder sagged in remorse, and he plopped onto the bed. He had failed Taylor. Failed Levi.

Images of Kyle filled his mind, the failure from that time returning like a wrecking ball devouring everything in its path.

"Wyatt, it's time for you to pay for your sins. Will you sacrifice your son?"

Wyatt gritted his teeth, breath hissing out in a razor-sharp stream. This was why Ridge hadn't killed him. He wanted Wyatt to suffer. Again. "Don't you hurt my son. Tell me where to meet."

"Good choice. Meet me at 0800 hours, where it all began. No cops or you'll find Levi's body floating in the Kesbush River. My hunters will know. Don't let your son pay like your dear Lisa did." Ridge ended the call.

Wyatt squared his shoulders, determination settling into every muscle like armor. He would sacrifice himself so his son could live.

It was the only way.

Taylor moaned and rolled her head side to side, struggling to open her heavy eyelids. Where was she? Dampness chilled her bones and cleared her dazed brain. She jerked her eyes open and sat upright, regretting her quick action as the darkened room spun. Taylor breathed in, waiting for the surroundings to still. After her vision leveled, she observed her situation. A dim pencil line of light sliced through a crack in the boarded-up window to her right. Whoever kidnapped her left her in a small cabin. She stiffened. Shadow.

She recalled him whimpering, and that she was about to get up to check on him when she felt the pinprick, followed by distorted voices talking about taking out Wyatt and nabbing Levi. More than one suspect had invaded Wyatt's ranch. Panic had struck her like a bullet through the chest, then darkness had blanketed her and swallowed her whole until only moments ago. *Lord, please help my boys to be okay.*

Her boys? Since when had she thought of Wyatt and Levi as "her boys"? *Since you let yourself fall. Again.*

She set the thought aside and wiggled her fingers, then her toes. Why hadn't they restrained her? "Levi, where are you?"

Silence answered.

Taylor must find Levi. If he wasn't here with her, where was he? And had the kidnappers taken out Wyatt like the voice had said? *Please God, no! Help him stay alive.*

She took another look around the one-room cabin, but she only noted dilapidated furniture—a couch, table, chairs, an older floor-to-ceiling stone fireplace. Her eyes settled on materials lining a long table on the other side of the room. Clamps, screwdrivers, wrenches and more. She gasped as realization dawned on her.

This was where they were modifying their weapons.

She had to escape.

Taylor swung her legs over the side of the cot, every movement slow and with purpose. Her legs wobbled, unsteady like a newborn colt. She waited, heart pounding, then took a baby step. Her knees buckled, arms thrashing until she caught her balance by using the rickety table to steady herself. Gritting her teeth, she floundered toward the door, using the furniture like handholds on a cliff.

She turned the knob. Locked.

Her heart rate pounded. She shoved her weight against the door, praying the wood was rotted. It didn't budge. Reinforced. Whoever kidnapped her knew they didn't require ropes—she wasn't going anywhere.

Or so they thought.

She grabbed a screwdriver off the table, waddled back to the boarded-up window and jammed the tool into the crack between the planks, pulling with all her might. Her head throbbed, her achy muscles yelled out in a silent scream, begging her to stop.

But she couldn't. She tugged again.

The planks held. No escape there.

Taylor dropped the screwdriver and slouched her back against the window, searching the cabin for another route.

Nothing materialized.

She slid to the floor, tucked her knees to her chest and rested her forehead as defeat overtook her strength. Taylor failed to protect Levi. Wyatt. Shadow.

The last words she spoke to Wyatt entered her mind.

I need a break from you right now.

Why had she said that? She didn't need a break from Wyatt Hoyt, but from her true feelings tumbling through her brain. She hadn't trusted herself, as she was about to reveal everything, including her love for him.

Tears cascaded down her cheeks like a waterfall emptying into a river at its base, expelling a flood of emotions. Tears of regret. Tears of lost love. Tears of bitterness over losing a father.

Bitterness she accused her mother of, but now realized she herself let the same ugliness enter her life. *You're a hypocrite.*

Flashes of memories plagued her—her father storming out of the house, letting the screen door slam behind him. Images of her mother exhausted and overworked, striving to make ends meet while leaving Taylor alone to fend for herself.

Next came her cancer scare years later. The silence that followed left her feeling neglected by the God she loved. He, too, had abandoned her. She was alone and barren.

Then, the news of her father's passing.

Taylor tensed, a clear picture dawning on her. All those circumstances had left her with a deep-seated fear of abandonment and trust issues, expecting everyone in her life to eventually leave. How had she not seen that about herself before?

She had done the same thing to Wyatt.

Her leaving him wasn't about the fact she couldn't have children.

Deep down she was scared Wyatt would leave her—and she couldn't face that.

So, she did what she was taught.

She ran.

Just like her father.

She failed Wyatt, Levi, Shadow, God—and herself.

Taylor deserved to be here, alone in a cabin without a way of escape. She deserved punishment. *You should have known better.* Just like in her childhood. Her father told her she didn't deserve his love before he walked out.

She wrapped her arms around her folded legs and sobbed uncontrollably until one word plunged into her mind.

Surrender.

Taylor gasped, her tears ending.

No. Her father's abandonment wasn't her fault. Neither was being kidnapped. She also realized she must release her bitterness toward her father. Yes, he left, but that and her barren womb didn't define her. God loved her for who she was. A child of the King.

God, I'm wrong. I didn't deserve to be taken. No one deserves that evil. Your love paid the price for me. Show me how You want me to change. I surrender to You. The only One who can erase my fears of abandonment. I trust You with my life. Mom's right. I must forgive my father. Will You help me do that?

Can you also show me a way out of this cabin, so I can tell Wyatt how I feel about him and Levi?

Please, God.

Rain splattered on the roof, bringing comfort. She had always loved that sound. It brought peace and washed away the anxiety coursing through her veins.

Thank You.

Taylor pushed herself to her feet and circled the cabin, searching for an alternate route. Her fogginess was slowly dissipating, so perhaps she missed something in her initial cursory check.

Rain continued to fall outside. A cluster of drops splatted into the open fireplace. *Wait.*

Taylor plodded over to the large rustic fireplace, showcasing its age in the jagged display of roughly hewn stones. Jutted at odd angles, they were stacked in an irregular pattern, leaving grooves between the bricks. She crouched low, stuck her head through the wide, soot-streaked opening, and peered upward. The same mismatched stonework extended into the old flue. Some bricks had crumbled and lay broken on the hearth. Dawn's light filtered through the open chimney, casting a glow on the debris. A ridiculous thought bull-rushed her. Could she climb out? Was this the escape she prayed for? Her tiny frame would fit, but she was in her bare feet. Running in a forest full of prickly bushes, rocks, twigs and creepy crawly creatures would prove to be a detriment to her well-being. But she had no other choice. She must try.

God, help this to work.

Resolve locked her muscles and filled her with courage. She dug out crumbled stone and other debris from the fireplace, clearing her way. Then crawled inside and placed one foot on a jagged brick, pushing down to test it. It held. She looked up and latched on to a brick, disturbing the stones. Dirt tumbled on top of her and she turned her head, waiting for the dust to settle before gripping a different brick. That one held, so she slowly began her ascent toward the rain clouds, letting the drops cleanse the soot from her face. Brick by brick, she climbed. *Almost there.* She caught ahold of the last brick and stuck her foot into a groove in the stones. Her foot slipped, and she clung to the brick she held. *Don't fall now.* She feathered her toes along the flue and found another groove, testing its strength. It held. She pushed herself up and out of the flue, climbing onto the roof.

She hissed out an extended breath.

You did it!

Relief flooded her body along with the heavy downpour, bringing a renewed sense of purpose. Time to find Levi.

She slowly stood, pushing on the roof. It held her weight. Good. Glancing around, she attempted to gain her bearings, but only saw trees. She was somewhere in Teragoose National Park.

Shouts echoed below.

She froze, then dropped back onto her knees. The hunters were coming for her. They would soon find her missing. Taylor held her breath as the door creaked open.

Run, Taylor.

Could she trust the rest of the roof? She didn't have a choice.

Taylor crawled to the opposite edge of the door to mask her escape.

Curse words from the hunters exploded as pounding footfalls revealed they had exited the cabin.

It was now or never.

Taylor gripped the edge of the roof and dropped down, clinging to the side. She looked over her shoulder to examine what lay beneath her. Bushes, trees, a woodpile. She shimmied to her right until she was above the bushes. They would at least break her fall.

This is gonna hurt.

She sucked in a breath, said a prayer and let go.

SEVENTEEN

Wyatt sped into Teragoose National Park station's parking lot, urgency fueling his every move. He'd stopped at his resource center long enough to grab his weapon. He wouldn't enter the forest without some type of protection. Supervisor Bain had been at the center early and caught Wyatt in the throes of gathering his Glock, a flare gun, flashlight, two sat phones, his duty belt and a concealed knife in an ankle holster. He demanded a reason why Wyatt was there and suiting up for battle. He was supposed to be off duty and hiding. Wyatt had given him an excuse that Cam required his help with an urgent matter. He guessed the mention of the man's favorite employee would put him at ease, and he was right. Bain backed down, but his tilted head and narrowed eyes warned Wyatt of the man's suspicions. He had hated to be dishonest, but he couldn't bring him into the mix for two reasons—Ridge had warned Wyatt against it and Wyatt still didn't know who to trust.

He checked his dashboard's clock. Six forty-five. Just enough time to make it to Kesbush Gorge if he took the park's ATV to the rocky incline. He'd have to proceed on foot from there. He prayed the rain wouldn't make the already treacherous path even more slick. *Guide my feet, Lord.*

Shadow barked from his cage in Taylor's K-9 cruiser. Thankfully, she had left her key fob on the kitchen island. Ridge had said no cops, but Wyatt guessed that he probably wouldn't consider the dog a police officer, even though technically Shadow was Taylor's partner.

Wyatt cut the engine. "Let's do this, Shadow. Ready?" he called over his shoulder.

Again, the dog barked.

Wyatt turned to face his father sitting in the passenger seat. Ridge had said nothing about Frank Hoyt. "Okay, Dad. You can only come as far as the Kesbush and Foxwick Trail."

"What? I'm coming all the way. You're not the only one trained in law enforcement."

Wyatt seized his father's arm. "No. Mom would never forgive me if something happened to you. Besides, I'm counting on you to bring Levi back down the mountain." Wyatt unhooked the sat phone and handed it to him. "When you see me shoot a flare, call Sergeant Bryan Mitchell of the West Newfoundland Constabulary and tell him what's going on. Only him. Taylor doesn't trust anyone else. He'll help us. Got it? Wait for my signal. I can't risk Levi's life."

Frank's lips quivered. "I don't want to lose you, son."

"Pray, Dad. Hopefully, God will listen to you."

"He will you, too. It's time to let go and trust."

Could he? Could Wyatt trust in God after all these years of heartache?

Wyatt opened his door and snatched his pack from the back seat, slipping his arms through the straps. "We have to move. I'll barely make it in time as is." He hustled to the back and released Taylor's partner. "Shadow, come."

The dog hopped down, steady and sure.

Thank You, God, for bringing Shadow's strength back.

Fifty minutes later, Wyatt and his father pushed their ATVs into the bush beside the Kesbush and Foxwick Trail, out of the view of Ridge's hunters.

At least, Wyatt prayed that was the case.

He cut the engine. "Shadow, down."

The dog hopped from his position between Wyatt and the ATV's handles.

Wyatt dismounted and pushed the ATV farther into the bushes. "Dad, bring yours in here, too. Ridge's hunters are ruthless and you need to stay out of sight, especially because I don't have a second weapon for you. Taylor had hers in a locked case. I couldn't get to it."

"Don't worry. I nabbed this from your kitchen utility drawer." He pulled a pocketknife out. "I wasn't about to come weaponless."

Wyatt resisted the urge to snicker. *Good for you, Dad.* "Remember, when you see a flare, call Sergeant Mitchell. And stay hidden."

"Got it." He tugged Wyatt into a hug. "I love you and I'm proud of you. I know I haven't said that enough to all my children. That's going to change."

Wyatt's throat clogged with a roller coaster of emotions. "Love you, too. Please stay safe."

"Bring back my grandson." His father retreated. "I want to see you, Taylor and Levi coming through those woods."

"I will do everything in my power to make that happen. Gotta go." Wyatt turned to Shadow. "Come."

The pair zipped through the tree line and veered up the rocky incline.

Lightning flashed through the trees, a blinding explosion that lit the forest a stark white. Thunder cracked a heartbeat later, and Wyatt flinched.

Perfect. Not what his son needed—

A deadly kidnapper and a storm ripping through the mountain pass like it had a personal vendetta.

Taylor ignored the pain stinging her bare feet and ducked beneath a cluster of trees to hide from the hunters hot on her trail. She rubbed her ankle, then rotated her foot to work through the pain. When she'd dropped from the roof, the bushes had broken her fall, but she landed hard on her right foot.

"Where is that girl?" The hunter's question blared nearby, indicating the men were gaining ground.

Taylor had to keep moving, but bolting from her hiding spot like a scared rabbit would reveal her position.

Thunder flashed, exploding light into the wilderness.

She cowered, jamming herself deeper among the bushes. *Keep going, hunters. Lord, make me invisible to them.*

"If we don't find her soon, Ridge will have our heads," one hunter said.

The other spewed a string of not-so-nice words. "And he told me he had special plans for the purdy cop."

Taylor grimaced and clamped her hand over her mouth to silence any further outbursts.

"Did you hear that?" The hunter stopped directly in front of Taylor's hiding spot, his muddy boots within reach.

She held her breath.

"Probably a squirrel. She couldn't have gotten this far. She's got no shoes on." The man snickered.

"Well, she climbed out of the chimney. She ain't stupid."

Move along, boys.

A radio squawked. "Ricky, meet me at the gorge. This boy is getting on my nerves."

Taylor tightened her hand on her mouth. Where had she heard that voice before? And he had Levi at the gorge.

"Copy, Ridge. Over and out." A pause. "Grizzly, you find that girl. Now! I gotta go." Rushed footfalls slowly faded into the background.

"Time's up, little girl. Come out, come out wherever you are." The other hunter clucked his tongue and retreated toward the cabin, whistling a menacing tune.

When his mocking melody dimmed into the shadows, Taylor waited a couple of minutes, then crawled out from her hiding spot. She ran in the opposite direction toward the sound of a rushing river, ducking in and out of the trees to conceal her presence. She must be close to the Kesbush Gorge.

Another flash of lightning illuminated the dim forest.

Thunder cracked, sending shudders throughout Taylor's now-soaked body. She shivered and continued on the path.

She stumbled on a cluster of rocks, piercing pain traveling up her leg. Ugh! Taylor dropped to the ground and held her throbbing foot. Her fingers grazed a sticky substance. Blood.

Not that she was surprised. Barefoot in the wilderness was never a good idea.

Father, protect my feet. I need to save Levi and find Wyatt and Shadow.

She eased herself upright and gingerly placed her wounded foot on the ground. She winced and jerked backward. *Come on, Taylor. You can do this.*

You have to do this.

She placed her foot back down, biting her lip to redirect the pain. She sidestepped the rocks and forged ahead toward the red bridge. It had to be where the other hunter had gone.

And where Levi was being held.

Loud voices farther ahead stopped her in her tracks.

"Cowboy is on his way. I threatened to send the boy into the river if he didn't comply."

Taylor covered her mouth with her hand, subduing any sounds she wanted to expel.

Wyatt was alive.

Thank You, Father. Protect us.

"He has five minutes." The voice's angered tone emitted an eeriness into the area.

A jolt surged through Taylor, sending a tidal wave of alarm crashing down upon her. She ducked into the forest and crouch-walked, tree to tree, to get closer to the voices. She had to be ready when Wyatt arrived.

She crept forward.

Then hovered behind a tree, waiting.

Watching.

And praying for a plan to strike.

* * *

Voices drew Wyatt's attention as he neared the Kesbush Gorge. He dashed behind a tree, keeping a tight hold on Shadow's leash. What was the command for him to remain quiet? He wracked his brain for the word Taylor gave her dog in the forest. Right. Silent. Wyatt squatted, bringing himself eye to eye with the K-9. "Shadow, silent."

The dog's ears twitched, and Shadow straightened, but remained silent.

His forceful but quiet command registered with the K-9.

Good.

Wyatt peeked around the trunk to assess the situation before revealing himself.

Fork lightning flashed across the gorge.

Thunder boomed.

A child's whimper filtered through the trees.

Levi.

He was scared, but safe.

For now.

Wyatt ducked back behind the tree. He needed a plan.

And fast.

Keep your eyes to the skies and your ears in nature.

His father's motto.

Wyatt complied, looking upward and stilling to hear nature's sounds.

The distant rumble revealed that storms surrounded the gorge. Not good. The rapids below told him the angry river would take no mercy. They must avoid the gorge at all costs.

Eyes to the skies.

Could his father have also been referring to God when he coined his motto?

Time to let go and trust.

Frank Hoyt's earlier words tumbled through Wyatt's head.

His father was right. Wyatt was tired of running not only from Ridge, but running away from God.

A melodic burst of whistles spilled from a mourning warbler above Wyatt's head. He looked upward.

Even in a storm, the tiny bird wasn't scared. It knew where to take refuge.

And now so did Wyatt. It *was* time to let go.

Time for Wyatt to surrender to the One who had sheltered him from storms. Sure, he'd had his share, but God had remained close, showing Wyatt the way.

Even when Wyatt refused to see Him.

Jesus, I'm sorry for failing You, but I know now You love me anyway. Even in my failures. My stubbornness.

Why had it taken Wyatt so long to realize that truth?

God never left, even through every crashing wave and storm that dragged Wyatt under. He'd been there, steering him away from the danger. Leading him through his troubles whenever the path took him straight into it. It was the only way to get to the other side.

Losing Kyle and Lisa had shattered Wyatt, leaving pieces strewn everywhere. Pieces he never thought he'd be able to put back together. But somehow, God had made him stronger. Softer. More compassionate.

Even so, Wyatt still clung to the past as if he could change the outcome. But he couldn't, and never would.

Time to accept that fact and give God control over his life, whatever time he had left. Beneath his fear of failures, his struggle to relinquish the reins—and yes, his anger—Wyatt held on to one unshakable truth—God knew what was best for him. And somehow…that *had* to be enough.

Lord, thank You for being my shelter in the storms. I see that now. I surrender my life to You. I release Kyle and Lisa to You. Levi and Taylor's safety to You. You have them in the palm of Your hand. Save them.

Thank You.

An image of Taylor snuggling close to his son on the couch entered his mind. God brought a new love back into his life and it was also time to share with her exactly how he felt, even if it was the last thing he ever told her. But right now, he must save her and Levi.

Wyatt unleashed Shadow but commanded him to stay.

He'd use Taylor's K-9 at the right time. Once he saved Levi, he'd use her uniform shirt he'd grabbed from her room to give Shadow a scent to find her.

Wyatt stuffed the flare gun at the back of his waistband, then withdrew his Glock and emerged from his hiding place. "I'm here."

A slim, bearded man sprang up from his position in front of a stack of crates. He whipped out a gun, his fingers fumbling to hold it steady. "Drop your weapon, Cowboy."

"Papa!" Levi's shaky cry threatened to be Wyatt's undoing.

Courage, Wyatt, courage.

Courage for him and his son. "Levi, you're going to be okay." Wyatt raised his gun and studied the man holding Levi.

The curly-haired redhead snickered and pressed the barrel of his gun into Levi's temple, his grip on Levi slipping. "You made it just in time." He sneered, revealing his yellowed, crooked teeth.

Something told Wyatt that neither of these hunters was the ruthless Ridge. "Where's your boss?"

Bearded man tilted his head. "Why don't you think one of us is Ridge?"

"Both of you are clumsy. Call Ridge. Now!" Wyatt held his Glock higher as he scanned the crates sitting beside the pulley system. State-of-the-art archer bows that reminded Wyatt of something he'd seen in one of Levi's superhero movies. The arrows didn't have the normal wooden shaft, but appeared to be metal. The fletching at the end of the bow was longer than most, the arrow head larger. Obviously meant to do major damage. The hunters equipped the rifles with machine-gun-like capabilities and silencers. No wonder Ridge tried hard to mask his empire. These weapons would make millions on the black market.

"Don't you worry about it. He'll appear when you least expect it."

Odd statement. Wyatt visualized Pete's map and inconspicuously examined the area, points on the drawing coming into focus. This is the spot the man had used for his map, but the row of x's still baffled Wyatt.

He took a step toward Levi. "Let my son go. Ridge promised."

"Put the gun down first," the bearded man said. "Or I will kill the boy." He pointed his weapon at Levi.

Wyatt raised his hands. "Okay." He tossed his Glock to the right. "I just want my son to be safe. Do with me what you want."

"Oh, I will, Cowboy," a voice said from behind.

Wyatt stiffened as the use of "cowboy" returned to his mind. Cam Field was Ridge?

Wyatt pivoted and came face-to-face with the ruthless leader, his jaw dropping.

Not Cam.

Hairs at the back of Wyatt's neck rose, sending an icy wave slamming through him—razor-sharp and paralyzing. "It's been you all along?"

The hunter sneered, raising his bow and arrow. "Yep. You and that pretty cop had no idea it was me."

How could Wyatt have been so oblivious to this man's evil plan all these years?

EIGHTEEN

Bushes rustled beside Taylor. Her muscles coiled, breath locking in her throat as her hand instinctively flew to her waist for her weapon. But nothing was there. She was still in her sweatshirt and plaid pajama bottoms. Had the hunter found her hiding spot close to the gorge? Something—or someone—was out there.

The bushes parted and Shadow appeared, knocking into her.

Taylor gasped and hugged her partner. "Shadow, you found me!" Relief flowed through her veins, loosening her tense shoulders until they sagged. "Thank you. Where's Wyatt?"

The dog let out a low woof and moved to the edge of the trail, glancing over his shoulder.

Taylor rose. Time to trust her dog's instincts. She promised herself she would never misjudge her K-9. "Lead on," she whispered.

Even though she didn't have her gun, she had her most powerful weapon—Shadow.

The pair trudged slowly through the forest and suddenly her dog stopped, emitting a low growl.

Then Taylor heard it.

Voices.

Specifically, Wyatt's voice.

She dropped to her knees and army-crawled under the bushes to be closer, with Shadow on his belly and sticking to her side. Taylor reached the opening of the Kesbush Gorge path, catching a clear view of the group.

Her cop instincts kicked in, assessing the situation.

A bearded hunter pointed his weapon at Levi, who was being held by a red-haired man.

Wyatt was facing her, but the man she guessed was Ridge had his back to her.

However, the strained expression on Wyatt's face revealed he knew the man, his shock evident.

"Let my son go." He shifted his stance, his eyes glaring.

He was preparing to strike, but Taylor realized that even if Wyatt could charge Ridge, the other two men would more than likely kill Levi.

And Taylor wouldn't let that happen.

A flash of lightning lit the dimmed region, glistening on something laying in the grass.

Wyatt's Glock.

She eyed Shadow beside her, a plan forming in her mind.

But it required the perfect moment to strike.

God, show me.

Taylor edged closer but missed the branch beside her. *Snap!* She held her breath and sunk her belly lower, but not before she caught a glimpse of the man named Ridge.

What?

"Where did you come from?" Wyatt shifted his gaze around the hunter to get a better view of what direction Ridge—aka Asher Calloway, the park's backcountry guide and outfitter—had traveled from.

Ash turned to Wyatt and sneered. "I'm shocked you never found the park's little secret."

"Are you referring to Pete Atkins's special map?"

Ash's eyes narrowed. "That man had the audacity to draw it so he could find it again. He bragged he concealed the entrance, but he'd caused too many problems and had to die. He was too greedy for his own good."

The row of *x*'s. "Don't tell me that his *x*'s did mark the spot?"

Ash peeked around Wyatt. "Boys, keep your weapons trained while I show Teragoose National Park's secret." He brought his attention back to Wyatt. "I lied. You're all gonna die anyway, so I might as well show you."

Wyatt inhaled sharply, a breath catching at the back of his throat. "You promised."

"Well, you had to pay for your interference. Apparently, Lisa's death wasn't enough. I'll let you watch my boys throw your son into the river. You'll have to face that cost. Then you'll die."

No! Wyatt clenched and unclenched his fists. He had to signal his father to get help, but how, without risking Levi?

Shadow.

Wyatt had to buy time. His gaze landed on the bushes behind Ash.

Wait? How was that possible?

Taylor was hiding in the wings.

Thank You, Father.

He cleared his throat to get her attention.

Her eyes met his, widening. She shifted her position and revealed her secret weapon.

Her four-legged partner.

Wyatt gave a slight dip of his head, acknowledging her.

Right now, he must turn the tables on Asher Calloway.

"Why, Ash?" Wyatt gestured toward the pulley. "Why go through such an elaborate restoration of the red bridge? Didn't you learn your lesson four years ago?" He realized his questions would anger the man, but that was what Wyatt was counting on.

Ash stepped closer, tension oozing out of him like a live wire. "You interrupted my ring four years ago. Your wife died because of it, and you're telling *me* I didn't learn my lesson?"

"How dare you cause her accident. Why not just kill me?"

"I wanted you to suffer because your interruption in my plan cost me dearly. I needed the money to help my baby sister."

"You have a sister?" Wyatt didn't really know Ash well, but he had always been friendly to him. And the campers and hikers raved about the man.

"Let me tell you a story, then I'll show you the forest's secret." He crossed his arms. "My dear old dad walked out on his family when I was eleven. Gigi was born nine months later. Mom struggled with providing for our needs, and she eventually died of a broken heart when I was seventeen." He placed his hands on his hips. "I had to take care of Gigi, so I took two jobs and eventually started selling drugs to stay afloat."

"So, this was all about money?"

He raised his hands. "Stop interrupting."

The man was indeed coming unglued and Wyatt had to let him in order to take control. "Go on."

"Gigi grew up and seven years ago announced she wanted to become a doctor, but we had no money for tuition. I couldn't resist my baby sister. She was all I had, so I came up with my weapon-smuggling ring, but first I needed help with modifying them, so I reached out and found a supplier on the dark web. He fixed me up with the materials and we made the adjustments at the old logger's cabin here at the gorge. No one used it any longer. It was then that I discovered the red bridge. It was the perfect way to smuggle the weapons out of the park using the Labrador Sea and Atlantic Ocean." He waggled his finger at Wyatt. "Until you ruined everything."

"So you hit Pause for a couple years to recalibrate your plan, coming up with the idea for the pulley system. How did you do that without attracting attention?"

Ash leaned his bow and arrow against a tree. He edged toward the thick weeds to the trail's right and squatted, parting the foliage. "We did it at night and traveled using the park's secret." He opened a door. "Take a gander at this."

Wyatt edged to the man's side and examined what Ash wanted him to see. "A secret entrance? Where does it lead?"

"Apparently, it was built years ago for moonshiners to hide and smuggle their brew. It winds around different paths and comes out about a couple of klicks from the park's main entrance."

Good, the man was now weaponless. *Keep him talking.* "What? So that's how you could come and go so easily."

Ash slammed the door shut and stood. "Yep."

"Why kill Denise?"

"She saw me kill Pete. I had to silence her."

Wyatt dug his nails into his palms to calm the anger bubbling inside. "And Levi?"

"Simple. I knew right away I had to use him to get to you, but in my rush to find your boy, I dropped my phone."

"And Levi hid it." He really was sick. "You killed Constable Day, but how with Hux nearby?"

Ash pointed to the tunnel. "Using this. I made up an excuse that I needed to make an important phone call." He harrumphed. "Hux never suspected a thing."

"I thought you loved Samantha."

His lips twisted into a sneer. "She was my eyes and ears within the station, but she just didn't know it. You see, I planted a recording device in her duty belt when she wasn't looking. It was how I heard about your girlfriend's conversation with Sergeant Mitchell. I was able to hack in and delete those records." He tapped his temple. "Clever, huh? But I needed the phone back, so she outlived her usefulness."

"What was so precious on the phone that made you kill her?"

"All my records. Mind you, they're all backed up on my server, but I couldn't have that phone falling into police custody. After Sam's death, I cloned your phone to monitor your activity and stay a step ahead of you. How else do you think I was able to bypass your ranch alarm?" He clapped his hands. "There, now you know all my stories. Time to die."

Lightning flashed, followed by a powerful thunderclap.

Ash jumped.

"Now!" Wyatt yelled.

"Shadow, get 'em!" Taylor's voice sailed out of the bushes. Shadow bounded toward the bearded hunter.

Wyatt unleashed the flare gun and fired, the flare shooting into the air.

Taylor cannonballed from her hiding spot and leaped to where Wyatt had tossed his gun. She snatched it up and held it toward the man holding Levi. "Set the boy down."

The hunter looked at Ridge as he backed toward the cliff's edge.

"Drop him in the river," Ash commanded.

"No!" Wyatt sprang toward the man.

He had to save his son, even if it meant sacrificing himself.

Terror slammed Taylor's chest as her thoughts spiraled out of control, grasping to find a way—*any* way—to save the two people she loved—Levi and Wyatt. She couldn't lose them. Not now. Not like this.

Shadow had subdued the one hunter, but if Taylor commanded him to attack the redhead, the bearded man would be free to strike. One plan of action entered her brain, but she'd have to get Wyatt to trust her.

Taylor prayed and raised her Glock. "Wyatt, drop!"

He obeyed.

She fired.

The bullet hit the man's leg, his hold on Levi weakening. He fell to the ground.

Wyatt scrambled toward his son and snatched him up into his arms.

A low, guttural grunt emitted behind Taylor. She swiveled.

Ash had claimed his bow again, getting his arrow ready to shoot.

"No!" Wyatt set his son by a tree, out of harm's way, and sprang toward Ash, knocking his body into the killer. The pair crashed to the ground and engaged in a brutal crocodile roll, wrestling for domination.

Taylor couldn't get a shot off. She wouldn't risk hitting Wyatt. Plus, they were too close to the cliff's edge.

Ash kneed Wyatt in the stomach.

Wyatt grunted and released his hold.

Ash sprang to his feet and fished an object from his back pocket, raising it high.

A detonator.

"I guess we all lose. If I'm going down, I'm taking you all with me. I rigged this cliff to blow." His finger inched toward the button.

Shadow barked.

Taylor pointed her gun toward the bearded hunter with her left hand and waved her right at Ash. "Shadow, get 'em!"

The dog barreled toward the man, latching on to his arm.

He dropped the detonator.

Wyatt hopped up onto one knee and pulled a knife from a sheath. "Taylor!"

She knew his intent but needed a clear shot. "Shadow, out!"

The dog released his grip and moved to the right in one swift motion.

Wyatt flung his knife toward Asher "Ridge" Calloway.

The blade lodged in the man's stomach. His eyes went wide—shock, pain and rage registering. He grunted as his knees buckled. He teetered at the edge for a second, then fell. His scream tore through the air with a ragged, eerie sound that echoed off the canyon walls until it faded into a haunting silence.

The other two hunters rose to their feet and staggered into the wilderness. They knew they were defeated.

Taylor pointed her weapon. "Stop!"

Wyatt drew her arm down. "Let them go. Police are on the way. My flare was the signal for Dad to call Bryan."

The adrenaline fueling her body dissipated, and she dropped to the ground. It was over.

Finally.

"Papa!" Levi raced to his father's side, Shadow following like a sentinel protecting his subject.

Wyatt opened his arms, and Levi ran into them. "You're okay. I've got you. You're safe."

Taylor waited for the pair to have their father-son moment. Their embrace warmed her heart, and she knew this was the time to tell Wyatt her feelings.

She now knew the truth. Even though she couldn't physically bear a child, she could still raise one.

Wyatt released his son and pointed. "Levi, why don't you and Shadow go sit over by that tree? I have to talk to Taylor."

"Shadow, come." Levi skipped toward the tree, the dog obeying the five-year-old's command.

Good boy.

Wyatt reached Taylor's side in two strides and dropped beside her. "Taylor, I must tell you something."

She placed her index finger on his lips. "First, I need to share with you something I should have told you two years ago." Her hand fell away and rested on her abdomen. "When I was younger, I developed cancer. Cancer that ended in a hysterectomy."

His eyes widened. "I'm so sorry."

"Wyatt, I broke up with you because I can't have children. When I woke up after my surgery, the doctor told me the news. I sobbed for weeks because my deepest longing was to feel a baby kick in my tummy and I would never get that chance. My sense of value died that day, so I promised myself that I would never marry, but then you came along. I fell hard and fast after our first date." She gulped to catch a breath. "When you started talking about wanting lots of kids like your large family, I panicked. I can't give you that."

His expression shifted, a gentleness settling on his face. "I don't care. We can adopt, you know. I'm sorry you can't bear a child, but God loves you for who you are. Don't you know that?"

"I do now, and I also know that my father's absence made

me a bitter person. I've given that over to God. Are you trusting Him now?"

"Yes." He caressed her face, his fingers grazing her skin, lingering like a whisper of hope. "I want you in my life. I love you, Taylor Grant."

She brushed his stubble, memorizing every line of his chin. "I love you, too, Cowboy."

He smiled, then closed the distance as his lips captured hers with a kiss that stole her breath. She let out a soft cry, not from surprise, but from the way her heart melted. She was here on the mountaintop with the man she loved, even though a storm raged around her.

She leaned into him, clinging to the moment as if nothing else mattered.

A moment reinforcing a truth—God clearly was in every storm of life.

EPILOGUE

Thanksgiving Day, eighteen months later

Wyatt held the door for his wife and waited for her to enter the ranch, where they'd celebrate their first Thanksgiving Day together as a married couple. Along with Frank and Erica Hoyt and Terri Grant. The smell of roasting turkey filled the air and Wyatt breathed in deeply. He'd always loved this special occasion, and today it held more meaning than ever. Renewal. Hope. Freedom.

He reflected on the past eighteen months. Sergeant Bryan Mitchell and his constables had rounded up all of Ridge's hunters, arresting them. They were serving time in a local prison. Park Warden Huxley Price had found his backcountry guide's body later that day. The shock of Asher's betrayal—and death—hit the park employees hard. He'd been well loved.

Constable Samantha Day's family held her funeral three days after the final showdown at the Kesbush Gorge. Her family had set up a foundation for grieving families in her memory.

Lisa's family and friends held a small celebration of life for Denise. It had been tough, but their love for each other helped pool their combined strength, giving God the glory.

Taylor and her mother had spent time together, mending their estranged relationship. Their mother-daughter bond was stronger than ever, and Taylor had worked through the loss of her father. She realized forgiving him was the only way to release her bitterness. It hadn't been easy, but she'd done it.

As for Asher "Ridge" Calloway's sister, Gigi? She'd been shocked to discover that her brother had funded her medical degree with illegal money, but she vowed to use her skills to save lives even though Ash had taken many.

Danger had entered Teragoose National Park, but peace had once again returned to the wilderness, breathing life into the forest and mountainous area.

The pitter-patter of tiny feet entered the hallway, drawing Wyatt's attention back into the room.

"Where's my sister?" Levi's gaze fell to the bundle Taylor held.

Shadow's claws clicked on the hardwood and he stopped beside the now six-year-old as if also wanting a glimpse.

"Mom, Dad, Terri. Where are you?" Wyatt wanted to share their new treasure with all of them at once.

His father appeared from the living room, holding a newspaper.

Taylor's mother ran down the stairs and into the foyer. "Is she here?"

Erica Hoyt scurried around the corner, wiping her hands on her plaid apron. "You're back so quickly."

Wyatt turned to Taylor. "Mrs. Hoyt, are you ready to show them our daughter?"

"Yes, my love." Taylor's eyes sparkled in the hallway's light. She set the carrier down, unbuckled the straps and lifted the two-day-old baby from her portable bed.

Wyatt and Taylor had begun adoption proceedings as soon as they were married a year ago. The lawyers put them in touch with an agency to help search for a baby. Everything happened much quicker than they expected, but they both knew it was all God.

He had provided them safety in the storm and given them another child. For that, Wyatt was thankful. Today was the perfect day to celebrate the newest member of the Hoyt family.

His mom leaned in. "What did you end up naming my granddaughter?"

Taylor's gaze snapped to Wyatt's. "You tell them." She handed their daughter to him.

Wyatt raised her. "Meet Kylie Erica Hoyt."

Kylie named after Wyatt's brother, Kyle.

Tears formed in his parents' eyes.

"She's perfect." His mother leaned down and kissed Kylie's forehead.

Terri caressed Kylie's tiny face. "Yes, she is."

Levi bounced on his tippy-toes. "Let me kiss her, too!"

Wyatt chuckled and held Kylie lower.

Levi placed a loud smack on his sister's face. "I have a sister!" He clapped and turned to his grandmother. "Can we eat now?"

The group chuckled.

"We sure can. Everything is ready." Erica beckoned for them to follow. "Let's go."

After carving the herb-roasted turkey, Wyatt settled into the chair at the head of the table adorned with fall decorations. Candles flickered, adding a rustic charm and scent of pumpkin spice into the warm dining room. "Time for our special Thanksgiving grace. Let's hold hands."

His family complied.

"Ready?" Wyatt asked.

They nodded.

"Go."

"For the family we cherish, we thank You, Jesus, with grateful hearts. In bounty and stillness, Your grace is the thread that ties our family together and makes us whole. In Your name, amen."

"Let's eat!" Levi passed his plate to Wyatt. "Lots of turkey, Papa."

Wyatt smiled, his heart full as his gaze lingered on the precious family God had placed in his life, a reminder of God's love and redemption. Each face around the table was confirmation of His mercy and healing that only grew deeper through brokenness.

Proof that even after life's fiercest and darkest storms, beauty could rise from the shambles—restored, reshaped and, somehow… more radiant.

And for that, Wyatt was truly thankful.

* * * * *

*If you liked this story from Darlene L. Turner,
check out her previous Love Inspired Suspense books:*

Fatal Forensic Investigation
Explosive Christmas Showdown
Alaskan Avalanche Escape
Mountain Abduction Rescue
Buried Grave Secrets
Yukon Wilderness Evidence
K-9 Ranch Protection
Danger in the Wilderness
Trail of Mountain Secrets

*Available now from Love Inspired Suspense!
Find more great reads at LoveInspired.com.*

Dear Reader,

Thank you for reading Wyatt, Taylor, Levi and Shadow's story! They had a treacherous escapade through the wilderness, didn't they? I enjoyed diving into the world of a conservation officer and setting this book in Newfoundland. Anything I embellished for fiction is totally on me.

As I wrote their journey through the never-ending danger in the relentless wilderness, one truth kept rising to the surface—God is with us in our storms. Wyatt's struggle to trust, Taylor's fight to protect and the K-9's unwavering loyalty reminds us all that faith isn't about having everything figured out. It's about holding on when nothing makes sense. I pray this story encourages you to trust in God's unwavering shelter in our darkest storms.

I'd love to hear from you. You can contact me through my website www.darlenelturner.com and also sign up for my newsletter to receive exclusive subscriber giveaways. Thanks again for reading my story.

God bless,
Darlene L. Turner

Get up to 4 Free Books!

We'll send you 2 free books from each series you try PLUS a free Mystery Gift.

FREE Value Over **$25**

Both the **Love Inspired®** and **Love Inspired® Suspense** series feature compelling novels filled with inspirational romance, faith, forgiveness and hope.

YES! Please send me 2 FREE novels from the Love Inspired or Love Inspired Suspense series and my FREE gift (gift is worth about $10 retail). After receiving them, if I don't wish to receive any more books, I can return the shipping statement marked "cancel." If I don't cancel, I will receive 6 brand-new Love Inspired Larger-Print books or Love Inspired Suspense Larger-Print books every month and be billed just $7.19 each in the U.S. or $7.99 each in Canada. That is a savings of 20% off the cover price. It's quite a bargain! Shipping and handling is just 50¢ per book in the U.S. and $1.25 per book in Canada.* I understand that accepting the 2 free books and gift places me under no obligation to buy anything. I can always return a shipment and cancel at any time by calling the number below. The free books and gift are mine to keep no matter what I decide.

Choose one:
- ☐ **Love Inspired Larger-Print** (122/322 BPA G36Y)
- ☐ **Love Inspired Suspense Larger-Print** (107/307 BPA G36Y)
- ☐ **Or Try Both!** (122/322 & 107/307 BPA G36Z)

Name (please print)

Address _____ Apt. #

City _____ State/Province _____ Zip/Postal Code

Email: Please check this box ☐ if you would like to receive newsletters and promotional emails from Harlequin Enterprises ULC and its affiliates. You can unsubscribe anytime.

Mail to the Harlequin Reader Service:
IN U.S.A.: P.O. Box 1341, Buffalo, NY 14240-8531
IN CANADA: P.O. Box 603, Fort Erie, Ontario L2A 5X3

Want to explore our other series or interested in ebooks? Visit www.ReaderService.com or call 1-800-873-8635.

---

*Terms and prices subject to change without notice. Prices do not include sales taxes, which will be charged (if applicable) based on your state or country of residence. Canadian residents will be charged applicable taxes. Offer not valid in Quebec. This offer is limited to one order per household. Books received may not be as shown. Not valid for current subscribers to the Love Inspired or Love Inspired Suspense series. All orders subject to approval. Credit or debit balances in a customer's account(s) may be offset by any other outstanding balance owed by or to the customer. Please allow 4 to 6 weeks for delivery. Offer available while quantities last.

Your Privacy—Your information is being collected by Harlequin Enterprises ULC, operating as Harlequin Reader Service. For a complete summary of the information we collect, how we use this information and to whom it is disclosed, please visit our privacy notice located at https://corporate.harlequin.com/privacy-notice. Notice to California Residents – Under California law, you have specific rights to control and access your data. For more information on these rights and how to exercise them, visit https://corporate.harlequin.com/california-privacy. For additional information for residents of other U.S. states that provide their residents with certain rights with respect to personal data, visit https://corporate.harlequin.com/other-state-residents-privacy-rights/.